MEDITERRANEAN DOCTORS

*Demanding, devoted and
drop-dead gorgeous—these Latin doctors
will make your heart race!*

Smolderingly sexy Mediterranean doctors

Saving lives by day…red-hot lovers by night

Read these four MEDITERRANEAN
DOCTORS stories in this new collection
by your favorite authors, available from
Harlequin Presents EXTRA October 2008:

The Sicilian Doctor's Mistress
Sarah Morgan

The Italian Count's Baby
Amy Andrews

Spanish Doctor, Pregnant Nurse
Carol Marinelli

The Spanish Doctor's Love-Child
Kate Hardy

CAROL MARINELLI finds writing a bio rather like writing her New Year's resolutions. Oh, she'd love to say that since she wrote the last one, she now goes to the gym regularly and doesn't stop for coffee and cake and a gossip afterward; that she's incredibly organized and writes for a few productive hours a day after tidying her immaculate house and taking a brisk walk with the dog.

The reality is Carol spends an inordinate amount of time daydreaming about dark, brooding men and exotic places (research), which doesn't leave too much time for the gym, housework or anything that comes in between. And her most productive writing hours happen to be in the middle of the night, which leaves her in a constant state of bewildered exhaustion.

Originally from England, Carol now lives in Melbourne, Australia. She adores going back to the U.K. for a visit—actually, she adores going anywhere for a visit—and constantly (expensively) strives to overcome her fear of flying. She has three gorgeous children who are growing up so fast (too fast—they've just worked out that she lies about her age!) and keep her busy with a never-ending round of homework, sport and friends coming over.

A nurse and a writer, Carol writes for the Harlequin Presents and Medical Romance lines, and is passionate about both. She loves the fast-paced, busy setting of a modern hospital, but every now and then admits it's bliss to escape to the glamorous, alluring world of her heroes and heroines. A bit like her real life actually!

SPANISH DOCTOR, PREGNANT NURSE

CAROL MARINELLI

~ MEDITERRANEAN DOCTORS ~

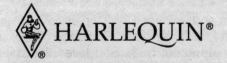

HARLEQUIN®

TORONTO • NEW YORK • LONDON
AMSTERDAM • PARIS • SYDNEY • HAMBURG
STOCKHOLM • ATHENS • TOKYO • MILAN • MADRID
PRAGUE • WARSAW • BUDAPEST • AUCKLAND

ISBN-13: 978-0-373-82373-4
ISBN-10:   0-373-82373-8

SPANISH DOCTOR, PREGNANT NURSE

First North American Publication 2008.

SPANISH DOCTOR, PREGNANT NURSE

CHAPTER ONE

'HAVE you seen him yet?'

Harriet Farrell had barely taken her jacket off before the question on everyone's lips was directed at her.

'I assume we're talking about the new consultant,' Harriet responded, rolling pale blue eyes heavenwards. 'I've already had two of the late staff waylay me and tell me how divine he is. And, no,' she added, turning to the mirror and pulling her straight, sandy red hair back into a ponytail. 'I haven't seen him.'

'He's divine,' Charlotte, one of the grad nurses, sighed dreamily. 'Spanish,' she added, as if that information alone was enough to exalt him to sex-idol status.

'Well, with a name like Ciro Delgato, even I'd managed to work that one out,' Harriet responded with a dry note to her voice. 'I just hope he's good at his job. Have you seen how full the waiting room is? Unless Dr Divine is as good as his résumé attests, we could be in for a very long night.'

'Oh, come on, Harriet, don't be such a killjoy. Anyone would think you didn't want to be here tonight.' Susan, one of the more senior nurses on the night shift, grinned. 'I'm as happily married as you are, but it doesn't mean that we can't appreciate a fine specimen when he comes along, particularly one with a dreamy accent! It certainly makes a night shift in Emergency go faster.'

'Ah, but you're not married to Drew Farrell, Susan,' Charlotte teased, not noticing Harriet's flaming cheeks as she rummaged in her bag for red and blue pens. 'I, for one, wouldn't want to leave my famous, good-looking husband alone in bed to do a Saturday night shift in this place, no matter how good-looking the new consultant was.'

It had been meant as a joke, Harriet knew that.

But even as she watched her colleagues head out for handover, even as she smiled and told them she'd be along in a few minutes, her throat was so thick with emotion she thought she might break down at any moment. Charlotte's comment had been so inadvertently near the mark it felt as if Charlotte must have read her diary.

Not that Harriet kept one!

Sitting down on one of the rickety plastic chairs, she allowed herself the indulgence of a few moments alone, letting the bright smile that was so much her nature slip for a while.

And she should have a lot to smile about.

Married to Drew Farrell, living in a gorgeous house in an exclusive beach-side suburb in Sydney, attending A-list events draped in the latest fashions. It was easier to smile and say that life was great than open up to relative strangers and admit the truth, easier to just carry on pretending that she and Drew were the perfect, golden couple.

If only they knew the truth.

Burying her burning cheeks in her hands, she let out a low moan.

If only they knew that 'happy' was the last word

she'd use to describe her marriage right now. If only they knew how hard it had been to paint on a smile and come to work tonight because they were desperately short of experienced staff. That just because she was married to a man whose name seemed to be on the tip of every thirteen-year-old's lips, just because the man that adorned teenagers' walls also shared her bed, it didn't automatically mean that life was wonderful. Standing up, Harriet stared into the mirror, every freckle magnified somehow, her snub nose scarlet now from her short emotional lapse. Even though the tiny mirror stuck to the wall with Blu-tack didn't reveal it, she could feel every lardy pound of overweight flesh digging into her waistband, could almost feel the incredulity behind the stares when Drew remembered to introduce her to his new friends. She could still hear the heavy silence that had resounded last night when she'd walked shy and un-certain down the stairs, draped from head to foot in a thousand-dollar dress, and the tiny beat of disappoint-ment that had resonated. Drew's eyes had told her that, despite the best designer, despite two months of mortgage money being spent on shoes, make-up and hair, she still hadn't quite looked the part of a certain actor's wife.

The look in Drew's eyes had told her that she looked every bit the fat night nurse she was…

'Stop feeling sorry for yourself.' Harriet said it out loud, forcing herself out of her self-imposed misery. After all, hadn't Drew been nice tonight? Hadn't he made her a coffee when she'd put down the telephone and told him that she'd be working an extra shift? He'd even filled her a hot-water bottle when a griping stomach pain had hit around seven p.m. and she hadn't been sure that she had been up to going in. He had tenderly rubbed her back and told her that she'd feel better soon.

He loved her.

She had to hold onto that—had to believe that the man she'd married, the man she'd believed in all these years, was still there under all the hype. That the dreams they'd built amounted to something.

'Thanks for this!' Judith Kerr, the senior nurse handing over the late shift, gave Harriet an attempt at a smile as she walked over. Having trained and worked in the military for a quarter of a century, Judith clearly couldn't quite come to grips with the rather more relaxed attitudes in civilian nursing and seemed to have a permanent air of disbelief about her. 'We're just so short tonight, not on numbers…' She gestured to the gathered crowd and didn't even bother to lower her voice. 'More on experience.'

'Thanks a lot,' Charlotte moaned, but Judith was unfazed.

'I'm here to run a department, not massage your tender egos. You might have read the textbooks, Charlotte, come top in all your assessments and exams, but until you've walked many miles in Emergency you need someone experienced to oversee the department. Now, Harriet might only have been here for a few months but she's been doing the job for years and, like it or not, that's what this place needs on a Saturday night! Especially when we've got a new doctor on.'

'How is he?' Harriet asked, far more interested in Judith's professional assessment than the dreamy whispers she had heard in the locker room.

'He seemed OK.' Judith sucked in her breath, which effectively meant 'but'.

'He was working his way through the patients beautifully at first, I was hoping to have the place a bit more ordered for you, but he went into cubicle four about an hour ago and has barely moved since.'

'What's the problem?'

'Nothing!' Judith said, clearly exasperated. 'There's a young head injury that needed to be discharged but instead of getting on, he's chatting away—even the patient's mother is getting impatient and wanting to leave.' Seeing Harriet frown, Judith explained further. 'The young girl studies classical ballet. Apparently she's really talented and, given that Dr Delgato has a "special interest" in sports medicine, he's decided to give her the five-star treatment.'

'Judith!' Even though it was a mere word, a single syllable, Harriet knew without turning her head this must surely be the new consultant. 'I would like to take some blood on this patient.' His thick accent was as deep and delicious as promised, but as Harriet swung around she was mentally knocked sideways at the sheer impact of Ciro close up. For once, the girl talk in the locker room had been woefully inadequate. Sexy didn't come close to describing him. Straight raven hair flopped over a divinely sculptured face, cheekbones razoring his haughty profile, but his delicious mocha-coloured eyes started to darken as Judith's tongue sharpened.

'*That* patient is a simple head injury who should have been discharged an hour ago,' Judith barked. 'You're not working at the sports institute now, young man. If she wants specialist treatment just because she's a ballerina, then a city emergency room isn't the place to get it.'

You had to know her to love her.

Had to know that behind that rather rigid exterior beat a heart of solid gold.

And even if Harriet had only known Judith a few short months, she'd met many Judiths in her time. Women whose barks were far, far worse than their bites. Old-school nurses who thought anyone under the age of fifty were just babies who needed to be told.

But whatever mould Judith came from must have broken when it hit the Mediterranean because clearly no one had spoken to Ciro like that before. His brown eyes were almost bulging now, his expression utterly incensed, and Harriet almost felt herself bracing for an impact, half expected a tirade of Spanish expletives to fill the emergency corridor. But even if his voice was controlled when it came, even if his stance remained utterly composed, the force of his angry glare, the slight twist of his lips as the staccato words came out had even the formidable Judith withering a touch under his direct stare.

'*All* my patients get special treatment, Sister. So do not even attempt to insinuate—'

'I was merely pointing out—' Judith attempted, but Ciro curtly shook his head.

'Are you on duty in the morning?' he demanded, waiting until Judith finally nodded.

'Then you should be very grateful to me. Very grateful that you are not the sister in charge when a fifteen-year-old girl who was discharged from your department the previous night comes in either in a state of collapse or cardiac arrest! I will take care of this by myself.' Stalking off, he left Judith, probably for the first time in her nursing career, standing open-mouthed and blushing.

Handover was rapid. Judith was unusually subdued and the rest of the day staff were no doubt keen to escape for the last few hours of Saturday night. When it was over Harriet took a few moments to allocate the staff beneath her, first asking if anyone had any preferences.

'Resus,' Charlotte immediately asked, and Harriet gave a small grin at her enthusiasm.

'You can work in there, with Susan,' Harriet agreed, keen to give the grad nurse the experience she needed, but ever mindful of staff-patient ratios. 'But when it's quiet, you'll need to give a hand out in A bay.'

'Louise.' Harriet gave an apologetic grimace, knowing that most emergency nurses wanted to be in where the action was, not watching from a glass booth in the waiting room. 'Do you mind covering Triage for the first part of the night? I'll make sure that I rotate staff.'

'Fine,' Louise agreed with a not too thinly disguised sigh, which Harriet chose to ignore. As the senior nurse on duty she needed to be on the floor and needed to delegate the staff appropriately, and Triage was important. As the first port of call for patients it needed a perceptive, experienced nurse to assess the patients and categorise them. As much as most nurses hated being in there, it was one of the most important roles in a well-run emergency department and a leaf or two out of Judith's book wouldn't go amiss.

Judith!

After a quick check to make sure everything was in order, Harriet headed for the changing room and, sure enough, there Judith was, slowly emptying her locker, filling her wicker basket with her Thermos and sandwich container, her proud face not even looking over as Harriet slipped in quietly.

'Judith?'

'I'm fine.'

'I know you are,' Harriet started, not quite sure how

to broach this difficult, proud woman but knowing she was hurting. Knowing that, unlike the rest of the mob who had scampered off after handover to the pub or their families, Judith would be going home to an empty house and that the only part of the shift she would remember was the final part. 'Look, in a couple of weeks you two will probably be friends,' Harriet ventured, and Judith gave a tired nod.

'Probably. Oh, Harriet, I didn't mean to imply that he was giving her preferential treatment just because she was a dancer.'

'No, you probably didn't.' Harriet gave a half-smile. 'But that *was* what you said, Judith, and, given it's his first shift in Emergency in this country and English isn't his first language, and given that your sense of humour doesn't come with a user manual, he'd be forgiven for thinking that you meant it.'

After the longest time Judith nodded, even managed a watery smile. 'Should I apologise?'

'Heavens, no!' Harriet gave a far wider grin this time. '*Never* apologise to a doctor, Judith, you know that better than me.'

Heading back to the department, happy that Judith wasn't if exactly cheered at least feeling a bit better, Harriet eyed the whiteboard, planning her next move. She wasn't sure what reached her senses first, the deep voice or the heady scent of his aftershave, but for reasons she couldn't even begin to fathom, every sense was on high alert as an all-too-familiar request met her ears.

'Who is in charge?'

Harriet felt her confident introduction dissipate into a croak.

'That would be me,' she somehow managed, dragging her eyes upwards. Incredibly tall, he was easily a good few inches taller than Drew who stood at six-one, but there was nothing remotely slender about him. Ciro was an absolute brute of a man, impossibly wide shoulders, the short-sleeved theatre blues displaying muscular forearms, dusted with dark hairs. Even his hands, holding out a casualty card towards her, were somehow sexy—olive-skinned and long-fingered. Harriet immediately felt incredibly guilty for even noticing they were utterly devoid of a wedding ring.

'The sister who was on before was very dismissive, but I am *preocupado*...' Ciro hesitated. 'Worried,' he corrected, and even though she'd already guessed what he was alluding to she gave a small appreciative nod when he translated his word effectively. 'Very worried and concerned about this patient.'

Grateful for something to concentrate on other than this divine specimen, she took the casualty card and skimmed through the notes written by the evening doctor Ciro had taken over from, cutting through the medical jargon in a moment and summing up the bare facts. 'Alyssa Harrison, fifteen years old. Fell at a ballet rehearsal, lacerated scalp, sutured, neuro obs stable, ready for discharge. What's concerning you, Doctor?'

'A lot, I think.' His voice was serious, and he gestured to an empty cubicle. 'Can I speak with you for a moment?'

'Of course!' Harriet agreed, but nothing was that simple in Emergency. Before heading off, she flagged down a passing RN with the words, 'I won't be long,' and, handing the drug keys to Susan, she added, 'Dr Delgato wants a word in private.'

'Lucky thing.' Susan grinned. 'Take as long as you need—I would.'

Thankfully the short walk allowed her blush to fade. No man had even come close to causing such a reaction in her and Harriet didn't even need to glance at the ring that adorned her own finger to know that whatever she was feeling was inappropriate.

'It would appear straightforward.' Ciro wasted no time getting to the point. 'Alyssa was seen and stitched before I arrived on duty—she had no neurological signs, etcetera, but the doctor who saw her suggested we keep her in for a few hours for head-injury observations, which have all been normal. Now her mother is very keen to get her home.'

'But?' Harriet asked, because clearly there was one.

'I don't think this young girl is well at all, I'm not happy to discharge her, yet she doesn't want to get undressed for a full examination,' Ciro said grimly.

'A lot of fifteen-year-olds wouldn't,' Harriet ventured, 'especially…' Her voice trailed off, but in the interests of patient care she cleared her throat and boldly continued, 'Well, you're a young man, good-looking—'

'I have taken that into consideration,' Ciro broke in, apparently not remotely embarrassed by Harriet's rather personal observation. 'She is swathed in legwarmers and a cardigan. All I have managed is to roll up her sleeve, check her blood pressure and take a small look at her ankles while I checked her reflexes. That was enough for me to see that this girl is not just thin, but I would say anorexic and severely malnourished. Her ankles are swollen and oedematous, which would suggest severe malnutrition, and her arms are very thin. Now, usually you would have the parent helping, telling the child not to worry, that it is a doctor examining her and this needs to be done, but instead the mother is agreeing with the daughter when she says that she doesn't want to get undressed and loudly insisting that any further investigations are unnecessary and that she wants to take her home.'

'OK.' Harriet chewed her bottom lip as she realised the possible gravity of the situation, listening intently as Ciro continued.

'I took her pulse for a full five minutes and she is having arrhythmias. I suggested that we put her on a monitor and do an ECG and some bloods, but the mother again refused. She said that she would take her to the family doctor tomorrow. It is my belief that the mother knows her daughter is grossly underweight, knows that if she is examined properly she will be kept in hospital, and is trying to avoid it.'

'Have you managed to speak to Alyssa alone?'

'No.' Ciro shrugged, his shoulders moving just a fraction. 'Sister…'

'Harriet,' she corrected automatically.

'Harriet, I do not overreact.' He stared unblinkingly at her. 'I do not make problems when there are none. I have asked for the most senior nurse to come with me, as I am going to attempt again to examine Alyssa properly, and if the mother again refuses then I am going to have to get…' Again he paused, again Harriet guessed he was trying to find the right word—only this time she attempted to help him.

'Heavy?' Harriet suggested, and from his slightly bemused expression clearly that wasn't the word he'd been searching for!

'If the mother doesn't comply, then the polite requests and friendly small talk ends and I will call the mother into the interview room and tell her that unless the daughter is examined and treated properly tonight, not only will I be consulting with the paediatrician but also the Department of Community Services, because, although it may be unusual circumstances, Alyssa is at risk.'

'You'll get *heavy*!' Harriet summed up for him with a smile.

'Very!' Briefly he smiled back as the alternative meaning of the word dawned on him, but it faded quickly, his voice slightly urgent when he spoke. 'Harriet, this is not good.'

She believed him.

Despite the fact she hadn't even observed him with a patient, had only known him for a few moments, Harriet knew, as nurses just did, that this was a voice of experience talking, knew to go along with his hunch in the knowledge it would be reciprocated; that one day when it was Harriet that was concerned, that when everything on paper told her that the patient was fine, she'd be able to turn to him and tell him that today or tonight or whenever the time came to follow a hunch, she was worried about a patient.

And he would listen.

'Let's go and get Alyssa examined and speak with Mrs Harrison, shall we?'

'Are you OK, Harriet?' He was still frowning. 'You look a bit…flushed.'

She *felt* a bit flushed, only, unlike earlier, it had nothing to do with six feet four of Mediterranean hunk and everything to do with her stomach pain which, despite a hot-water bottle and some painkillers, was still making itself known, but she certainly wasn't about to tell Ciro that.

'I'm fine.' Harriet shook her head dismissively, walking briskly towards the cubicles, ignoring the griping pain in her stomach and mentally preparing for the potentially unpleasant task ahead.

But Ciro clearly hadn't quite finished. One hand caught her arm as she went to go, those observant eyes staring down at her, narrowing slightly as he took in the pale lips in her flushed face and the tiny grimace of pain as she swung around to face him.

'You are unwell.' His statement was delivered as fact, his eyes holding hers as Harriet's mind raced for some witty response, desperate to shrug off his attention. Sympathy was the very last thing she wanted or needed right now if she was going to get through the night but, given that she had no choice but to get through the night, Harriet decided to swallow her pride and ask this relative stranger for a bit of help.

'I'm feeling a bit nauseous,' she admitted. 'Would you mind writing a script for some Maxalon for me?' She watched as his eyes narrowed slightly. 'I don't usually ask things like this, anyone will tell you that, if I could just have something to get rid of the nausea…'

'Fine.' He gave a short smile and Harriet gave a relieved one. 'After I've examined you.'

'Examined me?' Horrified, her mouth dropped open. 'I just asked you to write me up for two anti-emetics, Dr Delgato. Most doctors—'

'Are you saying that doctors here are prepared to prescribe drugs without examining their patients?' Ciro questioned, his frown deepening.

'I'm not your patient, Dr Delgato,' Harriet pointed out. 'I'm your colleague.'

'Well, in that case,' Ciro answered in the same tight vein, 'the answer is no.'

'Then we'd better get on with our work,' she responded tersely, reclaiming her arm from his grip and walking towards the cubicle more determinedly now. 'If you can give me a couple of minutes alone with her

before you come in, I'll see if I can get Alyssa undressed so that you can examine her.'

'You won't get anywhere with the mother,' Ciro
warned.

'Just watch me.'

Smiling, Harriet breezed into the cubicle, introducing
herself to the patient who lay on the trolley. As Ciro had
said, she was swathed in legwarmers and a thick
cardigan. Her dark hair was drawn back in a small bun
and gorgeous velvet-brown eyes, huge in her face, were
blinking in confusion as Harriet produced a gown.
Without pausing for breath, as if the entire conversation
with Ciro hadn't happened, as if she had no idea that
the mother and patient were resisting treatment, Harriet
explained in clear terms what was going to happen.

'Mrs Harrison.' Smile still in place, Harriet faced
the well-groomed, heavily made-up woman. 'We're
concerned that Alyssa's heartbeat is rather irregular at
times, so I'm just going to pop her into one of our
gowns and then the doctor can examine her properly.'

'No!' Mrs Harrison's voice was firm, her bracelets
jangling as she went to grab at the gown, rouged lips
furious, but Harriet's smile remained intact. 'I've
already been through all this. I want to take my daughter
home.'

'Of course you do,' Harriet replied sweetly, 'but it
really is imperative that Alyssa be examined thoroughly.
Hopefully it's nothing serious, but, as I'm sure you'll
understand, Mrs Harrison, we can't just ignore an irregular heartbeat.'

'As I've explained,' Mrs Harrison snarled, 'on several
occasions, I'd rather my daughter was seen by our family
doctor. I'll take her there first thing tomorrow—'

'This can't wait till tomorrow.' Harriet's smile was still intact, but the slightly dizzy air to her tone had gone. Her voice was firm, holding the woman's gaze as she spoke. 'Your daughter has a cardiac arrhythmia.' Still she stared directly at Mrs Harrison. 'It *has* to be dealt with tonight. I'm going to get Alyssa into a gown and put her onto one of our monitors so we can keep a closer eye on her.'

And something in her unequivocal stance, something in her voice, must have told the woman that this was non-negotiable, and even though Harriet would never have forced Alyssa to undress, she demanded the mother's co-operation, told her with her eyes that this had to be confronted. Finally, after the longest time, she felt an inward sigh of relief as Mrs Harrison gave a tiny reluctant nod and turned to her daughter.

'Listen to the sister, Alyssa.'

'Harriet,' she offered, her smile softer now, her eyes kind as she approached the young girl. If Alyssa was, as Ciro suspected, suffering from anorexia nervosa then being undressed and exposed would be traumatic for her, and Harriet was determined to make the entire procedure as gentle and as unintrusive as possible, covering the young girl with a blanket as she helped her out of her clothes. Harriet had to keep her own emotions firmly in check as she briefly witnessed the stick-thin limbs. She talked in gentle soothing tones as she gently leant her patient forward to tie up the gown and even though there hadn't been much room for doubt, any that might have lingered was quashed as she saw the length of Alyssa's spinal column, vertebrae protruding, dry, flaky skin hanging off. Glancing up at Mrs Harrison, Harriet saw a flash of shock on the woman's face but she didn't comment.

Now wasn't the time.

'Well done,' Harriet reassured the girl. 'Now, these sticky things just go onto your chest, and it lets us keep an eye on your heartbeat.' Placing the dots and leads on Alyssa's frail chest, Harriet quickly covered her back up, before turning on the cardiac monitor. As Ciro made his way in he gave Harriet a brief appreciative nod when he saw that the family was now being more co-operative.

'Alyssa, Mrs Harrison.' Ciro smiled warmly. 'I know you are both keen to go home, but first we need to ensure that Alyssa is well enough. Now, I know you've already been through this, but, given the doctor that first treated you has gone home now, can you tell me again what happened this evening when you cut your head?'

'I was at rehearsal—we've got the first performance next Saturday.' It was the first time Harriet had heard Alyssa speak, her voice, small and breathless, almost drowned out by the busy background noise of the emergency department.

'She's the lead,' Mrs Harrison explained. 'That's why I want to get her home. She needs her sleep so she can practise tomorrow. It's a very demanding role—'

'Alyssa,' Ciro broke in, 'why did you fall?'

'She landed awkwardly…' Mrs Harrison started, but her voice trailed away as Ciro and Harriet both looked at Alyssa for the answer.

'I was halfway through my routine and I just got a bit dizzy. It only lasted a second, but I was in the middle of a jump, so I fell awkwardly.'

'How often do you get dizzy?' Ciro asked, and Harriet could only admire his questioning, assuming, as was probably rightly so, that this was probably fairly normal for Alyssa.

'A bit…' She gave a tiny shrug.

'OK.' Ciro nodded. 'Alyssa, I'm going to examine you, it's nothing to worry about, and then I'm going to take some blood from you. Harriet has put you onto one of our heart monitors so that we can see what your heartbeat is doing and maybe find out why you've been getting dizzy.'

Infinitely reassuring, still he was commanding, his voice firm but somehow soothing. His hands were gentle as he first pulled down Alyssa's lower eyelids, examining the conjunctiva, then her hands and nail beds. Lifting the blanket and checking her reflexes, his middle finger probed the swollen ankles that looked out of place on such thin legs.

'You have some fluid retention. Does this happen often?'

'Sometimes,' Alyssa answered, 'but Mum gives me—'

'Just some vitamins,' Mrs Harrison said quickly. 'I get them at the chemist.'

'OK.' Ciro didn't push for any further details, acted as if the information barely merited a comment, but Harriet knew, just knew, it had been noted, but that for now he was focussed on the important task of gaining Alyssa's trust.

He listened to her chest, warming the stethoscope in his palms first, all the while keeping as much of Alyssa covered as possible. When he'd finished listening he probed her abdomen for a moment before replacing the blanket.

'Thank you, Alyssa. I know that wasn't pleasant for you, but it was necessary. I'm going to take some blood now. I'm going to insert a small cannula and leave it there, but from that I can take blood, and if we need to give you any fluids or medication we can do it all through there, so at least you'll only get one needle. I'll try not to hurt you.'

He didn't. Slipping the needle in neatly, he collected several vials of blood before unclipping the tourniquet and flushing the bung to keep it patent with the heparin flush Harriet had pulled up. Only when the blood had been taken, when the IV was in and Alyssa attached to a monitor did he approach the most difficult part of the whole subject. 'How much do you weigh, Alyssa?'

'I'm not sure…'

'Would you get the scales?' Ciro asked Harriet.

'Alyssa knows her weight,' Harriet responded without looking up at him, keeping her eyes on Alyssa. It would be easy to go and get the scales, but Harriet also knew that the delay and interruption could ruin the relatively compliant mood that they had somehow managed to foster, and it would be far better to forge ahead while the going was good. So instead she broached her patient, knowing, somehow *knowing*, this was what Ciro wanted her to do. Effective interview skills in Emergency required as much teamwork and synchrony as a surgeon and scrub nurse required, and with some doctors it took for ever—if ever—to perfect, yet with Ciro they fell into it easily, Harriet handing him the metaphoric scalpel without him needing to ask for it. 'How much do you weigh, Alyssa?'

'Forty kilos.' When still Harriet held her gaze, she answered again. 'Thirty-eight and a half.'

Deliberately Harriet didn't flinch and she was thankful that, when Ciro spoke, his voice was matter-of-fact.

'We'll need to check it before we give any medication,' he said, more to Harriet, 'but whatever way you look at it, this is very underweight.'

'She's a ballet dancer.' Mrs Harrison's voice was terse. 'She *has* to watch her weight.'

'Of course.' Ciro nodded, smiling at the agitated woman. 'But Alyssa is *extremely* underweight. I'm going to run some tests and then I'll ask one of my colleagues to come down.'

'And how long is that going to take?'

'It might take a while,' Ciro admitted, 'but I will tell you that it is my belief that Alyssa needs to be admitted—'

'No!' Furiously Mrs Harrison shook her head. 'This can all wait.'

'I'm afraid not.' Ciro shook his head. 'Look, I understand—'

'No, Doctor, clearly you don't!' Mrs Harrison angrily interrupted. 'My daughter is dancing next week in a role that could see her getting into the most elite dancing school in Australia. She has to rehearse, she has to—'

'Perhaps we could talk outside,' Harriet suggested, anxious to move what could be a very emotional discussion well away from Alyssa's bedside, but Mrs Harrison wasn't going anywhere.

'Perhaps we can't!' she smartly retorted, and Harriet knew that for now the conversation was over. 'I'll wait for those blood results, and then I'm taking my daughter home.'

'Thank you for your help in there.' Ciro caught up with Harriet at the nurses' station as Harriet attempted to put to paper what had just taken place, knowing that a detailed record, though always required, was especially important in cases such as this, so that the staff that were involved later knew exactly what had been broached and what the response had been. 'You were very good with Alyssa, the mother, too. It looked as if you actually knew what you were doing.' He smiled as she frowned. 'That came out wrong, forgive me. What I am trying to say is that you—'

'I worked on an adolescent psychiatric unit when I did my training,' Harriet explained, realising that no offence had been meant. 'I really enjoyed it. For a while there I even thought of…' Her voice trailed off, long-forgotten dreams briefly surfacing as she remembered the thrill of excitement at being accepted to study psychology and the thud of disappointment when her fledgling plans had been effectively doused. A part-time nursing wage, while she'd studied at uni, had been nowhere near enough to cover a very part-time actor, whose dreams had always somehow been more important than her own. But this was neither the time nor place for what could have been and, quashing memories, she concentrated instead on the matter in hand. 'Mrs Harrison was shocked when she first saw Alyssa undressed,' Harriet said. 'I don't think she knew, until then, just how thin her daughter was.'

'Because she doesn't want to know,' Ciro responded. 'At least, not until the concert is over and Alyssa has her scholarship. She wants her daughter to get into this dance school—that is her sole focus.'

'I think you're being a bit harsh.' Harriet frowned, but Ciro stood unmoved.

'I have worked with many athletes, and with their parents, too. Believe me, Mrs Harrison doesn't want to hear anything that might compromise her daughter's chances of performing next week, whatever the cost.'

His arrogant assumption annoyed her, and Harriet let it show, her forehead puckering into a frown, her mouth opening to speak, but Ciro got there first.

'I don't want them to leave the department.'

'We can't force them to stay—' Harriet started, but Ciro halted her with a stern gaze, his voice clipped when he spoke.

'I was not exaggerating earlier, Harriet. I will call Community Services if I have to. If Alyssa goes home, I can guarantee she will be back at the bar first thing tomorrow, rehearsing for her performance. And, from my clinical examination, it is my belief that that child is in danger of collapse and possibly sudden death if she exerts herself.

'So, I repeat—I do not want her leaving this department!'

As Ciro called over the porter and handed him the bloods to take directly to Pathology, Harriet stood stock-still at the desk, pen poised over the notes she was writing, her eyes shuttered for a moment. It wasn't Ciro's ominous warning that caused her eyes to close in horror, but the use of the word 'child'.

They were talking about a fifteen-year-old child, and she mustn't lose sight of that fact. It was their duty to protect her, especially if Ciro's educated hunch proved to be correct.

'What was all that about?' Charlotte nudged her, putting a massive pile of drug charts in front of Harriet that needed to be checked.

'The patient in cubicle four,' Harriet murmured, her mind ticking over. 'Alyssa Harrison…'

'The head injury that's here with her mother?' Charlotte checked. 'I thought she was being discharged.'

'Not any more. Ciro doesn't want her to leave the department. I'm going to ask Security to keep an eye on them.'

'But what if the mother wants to take her?'

'Then a simple head injury will become incredibly complicated.' Harriet gave a thin smile. 'Let's hope it doesn't come to that. For now just keep an eye open and let me know straight away if they show signs of leaving.' The emergency phone trilling loudly interrupted the conversation and had Charlotte practically dancing on the spot with anticipation. When the red phone rang, everything stopped! A direct line to Ambulance Control, it was used to warn the staff about any serious emergencies they could expect, and sometimes, if the situation merited it, an emergency squad of nurses and a doctor would be sent out.

Harriet answered the telephone calmly, listening patiently to Ambulance Control and shaking her head as Susan came over swiftly, with Ciro following closely behind, clearly wanting to find out what was coming in, or whether the squad needed to go out.

'Just a plane about to land with one engine,' Harriet said easily, and Susan gave a dismissive shrug, before wandering off. Even the easily excited Charlotte managed a rather bored rolling of her eyes and went off to answer a call bell.

Only Ciro remained, his expressive face clearly appalled at the news.

'One engine!'

'Yep,' Harriet answered. 'I'll just let the nursing co-ordinator know.'

'And then what?'

'Sorry?'

'Then what?' Ciro barked, clearly frustrated by her obvious lack of urgency. 'Am I to go out to the airport? Should we start moving patients out of the department?'

'Ciro…' Putting up her hand, Harriet stopped him. 'It's no big deal.'

'Tell that to the poor souls flying thirty thousand feet in the air,' he started, and somewhere deep inside, something flared in Harriet—a twitch of a smile on her lips, a small gurgle of laughter building within, a tiny flash of mischievousness at the realisation that she could prolong his agony, a glimpse of the old Harriet, the old, fun-loving Harriet, that seemed to have been left behind somehow. Ciro responded to it.

'What?' His lips were reluctantly twitching into a smile, too. 'What is so funny? I am overreacting, no?'

'Yes.' Harried grinned. 'You obviously haven't worked in an emergency department that covers an international airport before.'

'No.'

'Those *poor souls* won't even know there's a potential problem. This type of thing happens all the time. Ambulance Control alerts us as a courtesy, to be ready in case…'

'Then shouldn't we be doing something, getting ready?'

'Ciro, we are ready,' Harriet answered. 'The mobile emergency equipment was all checked at the beginning of the shift, we've got a major disaster procedure plan in place, ready to be implemented at any given moment. This is a fairly regular occurrence. Planes can and do land perfectly well with one engine. However, as a precaution, the airport emergency crews will all be ready to meet the plane and if, *if*, a disaster were to eventuate, we'd commence the major incident plan. But for now it's way too soon to do anything.' He didn't look particularly convinced. 'Ciro, if they had rung to say a plane was going to land with *no* engines, we'd be moving. This time next month you'll barely turn a hair at the news. They'll ring soon to say it's landed safely.'

He gave a relieved nod and she should have left it there, should have ended it with a swift smile and got straight back to work, but she didn't.

'Unless, of course, the wheels get stuck in the undercarriage.'

'Now you are teasing.'

'Yes.' Harriet smiled, but somewhere in mid-smile it wavered, somewhere in mid-conversation the witty responses ended and all she could do was stare. Stare back at those mocha eyes that held hers, stare at that full, sensual mouth. He smiled back at her and the terrible realisation hit that she was flirting.

Oh, not licking her lips and hand on hips flirting, but there was a dangerous undercurrent that was pulling her. A rip in the ocean that was slowly but surely dragging her in, this seemingly light conversation peppered with dangerous undertones. Surely, surely she shouldn't be noticing the tiny golden flecks that lightened those velvet eyes, surely she should no more than vaguely register the heavy, masculine scent of him. But instead it permeated her.

Harriet could feel her own pulse flickering in her throat and from the tiny dart of his eyes Ciro registered it too, and for a slice of time the department faded into insignificance, for a second it was only the two of them, not two colleagues sharing a light-hearted joke, but instead a man and a woman partaking in that primitive, almost indefinable ritual. A ritual that somehow acknowledged mutual attraction, that managed, without words, to voice a thousand questions. Never had she been more grateful for the sharp trill of the emergency phone ringing, dragging her back to reality, a mental slap to her flushed cheeks, a chance to regroup, to pull back, a chance to stop something that must never, ever be started.

'It landed.' Her voice was high and slightly breathless as she replaced the receiver, taking great pains to calmly log the call in the book, anything other than look at him. 'Safely.'

'I told you it would!' Blinking in confusion, she dragged her eyes to his, smiling despite herself when he gave a nonchalant shrug and somehow turned the previous few minutes on their head. 'Didn't I try and tell you that you were overreacting, Sister?'

One good thing about being busy was that the hours went by quickly. Ciro, clearly used to dealing with a full department, worked his way expertly through the patients. Harriet guessed that once he didn't have to pause to look up every last phone number and find out where every blessed form was kept to order various tests, he'd be an absolute dream to work with—so long as you followed his rules!

'Look at you, Harriet!' Charlotte's voice was almost a screech. 'You're in the newspaper! Why didn't you say?'

Mortified, clutching a telephone receiver in one hand, with the other Harriet reached out to grab the paper, but Charlotte was having none of it. At twenty-one she was a huge fan of Drew's and never missed an opportunity to talk about him.

'I just saw one of the patients reading it! I told them that you worked here so they let me have the paper— Oh, Harriet, you look gorgeous!'

'I look huge,' Harriet corrected, refusing to even glance at the beastly photo of her on the red carpet at the acting awards ceremony that had been held the previous night.

'Any results back on Alyssa?' Ciro asked as he came

over. 'The medics are waiting to see her, but I want some more information before I speak with the mother again and tell her that we're keeping her in.'

'I'm still on hold.' Harriet didn't even look at him, couldn't actually! She was concentrating too hard on breathing, tiny white spots dancing in front of her eyes, sweat beading on her forehead as great waves of nausea rolled over her. And Charlotte's incessant voice wasn't exactly helping matters.

'But you're not huge, you look stunning!'

'Who looks stunning?' she could hear Ciro asking, mortification heaped on mortification as behind her back Charlotte gleefully showed him the photo and took the new doctor on a whirlwind tour of her supposedly wonderful life.

'Harriet here is married to a soap star.'

'Soap?'

'Soap opera!'

'Her husband is an opera singer?'

'No, he's on TV. How come,' Charlotte asked with the tactlessness only a very pretty twenty-one-year-old could get away with, 'that with the patients your English is brilliant, but when you're talking to us it's—'

'Charlotte!' Harriet warned, putting her hand over the mouthpiece of the phone, but Ciro was unfazed.

'Because most of the English exams that I had to pass concentrated on medical terminology,' Ciro answered easily. 'I can name every bone in your body yet I cannot talk easily about television shows.'

'He could name every bone in my body,' Susan sighed as Ciro headed back to the cubicles, with Charlotte following like a faithful puppy. 'He's very good, isn't he?' Susan carried on, following Harriet's far-away gaze as she sat on the telephone on seemingly eternal hold, trying to chase up Alyssa's blood results. Despite marking the forms as high priority the results still hadn't come through and Mrs Harrison's already short fuse was clearly about to run out. Glancing over to cubicle four, Alyssa frowned as Mrs Harrison pulled the curtain, effectively blocking her view.

'He's doing well,' Harriet admitted almost reluctantly, determined not to let even a hint of what she was feeling carry to her peers, rolling her eyes as yet again the switchboard operator asked her to stay on hold. 'So long as you don't ask him for any favours.'

'Meaning?'

'Meaning I asked him to write up two Maxalon for me and he refused. He said that he'd only write them up if he examined me first.'

'And you said no!' Susan teased. 'I wouldn't have to be asked twice to take my kit off. Are you OK?' she asked more seriously when Harriet didn't smile back, just fanned her face with her hand and licked lips that were suddenly dry.

'No,' Harriet finally admitted. 'In fact, once I get these results I think I'm going to have to take first break. Susan, would you mind going and checking on Alyssa? Tell Mrs Harrison that we need the curtains kept open, unless she's using a bedpan, of course.'

'Sure.' Susan stepped down from her stool. 'And when I've done that do you want me to ring the supervisor, and see if she can send someone down to replace you?'

'Fat chance.' Harriet rolled her eyes. 'I was the last of the last resorts already. I'll just have to grin and bear it, I'm afraid. Let's hope the department stays quiet.'

Jinx!

Even as the words came out of her mouth, even before

the two nurses could touch the wooden desk in front of them in an effort to stop the jinx, the urgent call went up!

A loud crash, followed by a wail of horror filled the relatively quiet department and, throwing the receiver down on the desk, Harriet managed a rueful smile as she ran towards cubicle four, Susan quickly apportioning blame as she ran behind. 'That's your fault, Harriet!'

CHAPTER TWO

CIRO beat them there.

Pulling back the curtain and assessing in a split second what had happened, Ciro knelt down and swiftly examined Alyssa who lay unconscious on the floor. He checked her vital signs as Harriet pulled an oxygen mask from the wall and placed it over the young girl's mouth, careful not to move her until Ciro gave the OK.

'She said she felt OK,' Mrs Harrison was sobbing. 'I thought if I got her home to her own bed—'

'Did she hit her head when she fell?' Ciro's question was direct.

'No. She was just getting of the trolley and she went dizzy.'

'Did you break her fall?'

'Yes!' Mrs Harrison's voice was a screech. 'What the hell's happening? Has she fainted or something?'

That was what Harriet had been hoping when first she'd seen the young girl collapsed on the floor, but normally, with a simple faint, consciousness returned almost as soon as the patient was prone. But despite the oxygen, despite the seconds ticking past, Alyssa still lay unconscious.

'Let's get her over to Resus.' Ciro's expression was

grim as he attempted to check her blood pressure, but as Harriet went to pull out the trolley Ciro impatiently shook his head. He swiftly removed the oxygen mask. Picking up the feather-light young girl in his arms, he carried her through the department to the better-equipped resuscitation room as Harriet moved like lightning ahead of him.

'Fast-page the paediatricians,' Ciro ordered, but thankfully Susan was already on to it. Even Charlotte was thinking ahead, pulling open a flask of IV saline to run through a drip, but though Harriet was pleased to see her acting independently, she still needed supervision.

'Charlotte,' Harriet called, as she attached Alyssa to a multitude of monitors, 'run the saline through a paediatric burette. She's extremely underweight so we have to be very careful of doses.'

'We need to be very careful not to overload her with fluid,' Ciro confirmed and even though he was busy, inserting an IV and connecting the drips, he still managed to find the time to explain his thought process to the eager grad nurse. 'Her heart is beating irregularly, she may have some heart failure, so the last thing we want to do is give her more fluid than her heart can deal with. On the other hand...' He paused as he carefully examined Alyssa's neck, checking her jugular venous pressure. Then he whipped out his stethoscope and listened carefully to her lungs for a moment before resuming his knowledgeable lecture. 'She is undoubtedly dehydrated. Let's give her a stat 200 ml bolus. I want a catheter put in and her input and output strictly monitored.

'Come on, Alyssa.' His words were loud, the call to his patient sharp as he not-too-gently rubbed her sternum. It worked. Alyssa's eyes flickered open as she attempted to push him away. 'Good girl.' Ciro's voice was more soothing now, moving quickly to orientate his patient to her new surroundings. 'You lost consciousness again, Alyssa, so we have moved you to a different area of Emergency where we can keep a closer eye on you…' The frantic running of feet along the corridor outside heralded the arrival of the paediatric team, but instead of turning to greet them, Harriet noted with approval that he carried on talking to Alyssa, perhaps sensing that a full emergency team arriving at her bedside would be daunting for the young girl. Ciro took time to reassure her that, despite the apparent chaos, everything was very much in order. 'We were concerned about you so there are going to be a lot of doctors arriving and a lot of talk that you don't understand, but you are going to be OK.'

There certainly were a lot of doctors arriving. An emergency call always merited a rapid response, but the page had been put out as a paediatric emergency and though the difference was probably negligible, Harriet was sure that everyone had run just that bit faster to get there, from the anaesthetist to the nursing supervisor.

'Alyssa Harrison,' Ciro explained, 'presented with a head injury secondary to a fall while dancing…'

Harriet listened as she worked on, listened to his heavily accented English barely faltering as he explained Alyssa's complicated symptoms, and even though it was his first night, even though none of the doctors had met him before, he delivered his findings with a calm authority that demanded respect, explained without words to the rapidly gathering crowd that he was very much in control.

'Can you chase up those results?' Ciro looked over and Harriet let out a low moan.

'I've left the pathologist hanging on the line.'

'Tell him we'll be sending some blood gases along shortly,' Ciro called as Harriet rapidly headed back for the nurses' station.

It took for ever to get through, the switchboard operator telling her in a rather pained voice that 'yet again' she was about to be connected, but suddenly those tiny white spots that had been dancing in front of her eyes earlier seemed to have returned for an encore. The nurses' station seemed impossibly small all of a sudden. Sweat trickled between her breasts as she choked back bile, pleading with the powers that be to just let her get through the next few minutes of her life without major problems. If she could just get the blessed results down, she could hopefully escape the department for five minutes.

'Harriet, we need those results!' Ciro's voice was booming at her, his impatient face swimming before her eyes as she looked up. Finally Harriet conceded to herself that she had to get to the bathroom at once. Hurling the receiver somewhere in Ciro's direction, she stumbled off the stool.

'The pathologist is on the line now.'

'So, what are the results?'

'I don't know,' she mumbled, backing out, her hand over her mouth. Thankfully Susan was around, and recognised potential disaster before it hit. Susan's reflexes were like lightning, guiding Harriet to a vacant cubicle, sitting her on a chair and mercifully producing a bowl as she pulled the curtains on one of the many humiliating moments in Harriet's life!

CHAPTER THREE

'GIVE her the Maxalon, you meanie,' Susan teased as Ciro stepped into the cubicle a few moments later.

Thankfully his telephone conversation with the pathologist had at least given Susan enough time to remove the offending bowl and for Harriet to rinse her mouth and at least manage a semblance of dignity.

'I've already discussed this with Harriet,' Ciro said, completely unmoved. 'Now, will you let me examine you?'

'There's no need,' Harriet insisted. 'I went out to dinner last night, the food was really rich…'

'Did you have a lot to drink?'

'Apart from mineral water, no.' Standing, attempting not to wince with the pain that small exertion caused, she attempted a brisk smile. 'I'd better get back out there.'

'You are in no fit state to be working.'

'I'm much better now,' Harriet muttered.

'I disagree. I have already spoken with the nurse supervisor and she is arranging cover for you.'

'You've what?' Appalled, she glared at him. 'How dare you?'

'I dare because I am the doctor in charge tonight and I need my colleagues, especially my senior ones, to be

completely on the ball. There is no room for error in
Emergency.'

He was right, of course, Harriet knew that deep
down, but it didn't make her feel any better.

'Now, are you going to let me examine you?'

'No,' Harriet answered tartly. 'You should be in with
Alyssa, instead of worrying about me.'

'The paediatricians are in with Alyssa now.
Everything is under control.'

'Including me.' Harriet bristled. 'I'm going to wait
for the nurse supervisor to arrange cover and then I'm
going to take some paracetamol and lie down for an
hour or so until I feel well enough to start working
again.'

'You shouldn't take anything until you know what's
wrong with you. I'm not going to give you anything.'

'You really are the limit, you know!' Embarrassment
was turning into anger now, furious at his control, his
authoritative air—well, it might quiet his patients but it
damn well wasn't going to silence her into submission.
'Well, Dr Delgato, as it happens, I have some painkillers in my handbag, painkillers that don't require some
over-inflated doctor's signature to take, unless there's a
rule that's suddenly been invented that I don't know
about, unless I'm not allowed to go into my locker
without your consent, unless I'm not allowed to open my
bag and take my own tablets without your permission!'

'You are being childish,' Ciro responded, not
remotely fazed by her outburst. 'But as you're now off
duty, that is entirely your prerogative.

'Now, I suggest you put on a gown, lie down on the
trolley and rest for a while. Then, with your consent, I
will come in and examine you once I have spoken to
Mrs Harrison to let her know what is going on.'

She wasn't sure if it was deliberate, but the mention of the Harrisons made her protests about refusing to put on a gown and be examined rather feeble, childish even, and Ciro seemed to sense the change in her.

'How do you feel now that you have vomited?'

Which wasn't exactly the sweetest line to deliver a woman, but Harriet knew that his medical brain meant well.

'A bit better.'

'Good! Then rest and I'll be back shortly.'

She gave a reluctant nod. 'How are Alyssa's results?' She knew, just knew, he was about to shake his head and tell her that it was no longer her problem, so Harriet added quickly, 'I really would like to know.'

'Her potassium is dangerously low, as is her albumin, her renal function is decreased, she's extremely malnourished, which is why she has the peripheral oedema. I've spoken with Pathology and it would seem those *vitamins* that Mrs Harrison's been giving to her daughter are, in fact, diuretics, which of course are used to get rid of oedema, but that's the trouble with self-prescribing…' He gave her a tight smile as Harriet blushed. 'As you know, some diuretics need to be taken with a potassium supplement. Instead, Alyssa's potassium has dropped so low she is in danger of having a serious cardiac arrhythmia and possibly a cardiac arrest. I'll let you know how it goes when you're feeling a bit better.'

'Thank you.'

It was horrible, horrible, horrible being on the other side of the curtain. Horrible lying in a flimsy gown with the ties missing, on a hard trolley. Horrible having a probe stuck in your ear and your blood pressure taken, but that didn't even begin to compare to the humiliation of lying back and closing one's eyes while someone as divine and toned and clearly fit as Ciro told you to stop trying to hold in your stomach so that he could examine you properly.

She didn't even want to think about the *sensible* knickers she was wearing, supposedly safe in the knowledge she had been going to work.

'Tender?' Ciro asked as Harriet gave a stifled moan.

'A bit.'

'And here?'

'No.'

'Hmm.'

The dreaded 'hmm'—the sound doctors worldwide made as they broached a tentative diagnosis.

'You are tender in the right iliac fossa. I think it could be appendicitis or possibly an ectopic pregnancy.'

'I'm not pregnant.'

'Do you have your period?'

'No,' Harriet croaked.

'So when is it due?'

'Soon.' Blushing to the roots of her hair, she tried to focus on dates to respond to this necessary but excruciatingly embarrassing question in as matter-of-fact a way as she could muster. 'Actually, it was due a couple of days ago but—'

'Hmm.'

'I'm not pregnant.' Meeting his doubtful eyes, Harriet shook her head firmly on the pillow. 'I'm definitely not pregnant.'

'You are on the Pill?'

Harriet gave a small nod, hoping that would be enough to mollify him but knowing that it was futile.

'The Pill isn't always a hundred per cent effective.'

'I'm just not pregnant, OK?' Wrenching the beastly gown down over her stomach, she prayed for her blush to fade, prayed for this interrogation to end. 'So I haven't got an ectopic pregnancy and neither do I have appendicitis. I just want to go home to my own bed—'

'Harriet, I know that this is embarrassing for you.' Perching himself on the trolley, he took her hand, the touch so unexpected, so surprisingly tender she felt tears prick her eyes, his glimpse of kindness providing no balm, more a sharp sting to her bruised emotions. 'It is always awkward when staff are ill, but the fact is you have not looked well since you first came on duty and you are getting progressively worse. It clearly needs to be dealt with. Now, as uncomfortable as these questions are, they have to be asked. In a young woman, with abdominal tenderness, vomiting and a late period, it would be criminally negligent of me not to consider that it could be a ruptured ectopic pregnancy. So can you tell me why I should rule out that diagnosis? Are you unable to conceive, is there anything in your medical history…?'

And she didn't want to voice it, didn't want to admit it even to herself let alone anyone else, but knowing the truth was needed, drawing strength from the kind eyes that stared in concern, the warmth from the hand holding hers, Harriet let go of the horrible truth she had held in so tightly for so long now, admitted, perhaps for the first time, the hopelessness of her own situation.

'I'm using the only completely reliable form of contraception.' Swallowing hard, she forced herself to say it, to just get this the hell over with. 'Abstinence! I can't be pregnant because I'm not sleeping with my husband.' She saw the flicker of confusion in his eyes, second-guessed what was coming next. 'We haven't slept together for months now, not since Drew got this job and we moved to Sydney. So, you see, I couldn't possibly be…' Tears that had been held back for so long were now finally trying to come forth and holding them in hurt her ribs almost as much as the pain in her stomach did.

'You are allowed to cry, Harriet.'

'No, Ciro, I'm not.'

'You don't have to hold it all in,' Ciro insisted.

But she did.

Had for so long now it came as second nature.

'When David decided his name should be changed to Drew I had to grin and bear it,' Harriet snarled. 'And when Drew needs a pair of designer jeans for an audition I just work an extra shift, when he misses out on a part that should have been his I'm the one who has to deliver a pep talk…' The floodgates were opening now, years of suppressed anger bubbling to the fore, and she didn't care. For the first time in her entire adult life, Harriet couldn't give a damn about someone else's feelings. She blurted out her anger and frustration because it helped and, she decided, choking through her vented fury, he didn't have a clue what she was going on about. Her rapid spate of furious words was way too fast for him to understand.

All he had to do was hold her hand—which he was.

Nod at her very occasional pauses—which he did.

And give an occasional sympathetic murmur when her voice shrilled—rather regularly.

And through it all he didn't say a word, didn't attempt to say he understood as Harriet ranted on. 'Since he got this bloody job, I'm not good enough,' Harriet raged. 'Not thin enough, or demure enough, not quite the happening young metrosexual's partner.' She registered his frown.

'He is gay?' Ciro finally spoke.

'No.' Somehow Harriet managed a strangled gurgle of laughter. 'Metrosexual, it's the buzz word for today's kind of man. A man who doesn't mind admitting he takes care of himself.'

His frown only deepened.

'He has facials, dresses well, has his hair coloured, his eyebrows...' Her voice petered out.

'*And* he doesn't sleep with you?' There was just a hint of innuendo to his voice that really wasn't helping matters.

'He's under a lot of pressure at the moment,' Harriet offered in her husband's defence. 'He has to get up at the crack of dawn for early shoots, it's the only time the beach is empty.'

Which mollified him not! Clearly the Spanish didn't need a full eight hours in the cot for a performance! Clearly the Spanish didn't give a hoot about eyebrows and waxing and face creams. And it would have been so much easier if Ciro was ugly. If his eyebrows joined or he smelt of garlic, if she could just somehow eke out a hint of justification as to why Drew needed to spend so much energy and money to be a man, when this very unpampered male sat opposite her.

'I'm sorry!' She gave a rather ungracious sniff. 'If it was embarrassing before, it positively—'

'It's fine.' He smiled. 'You're not the first patient I've had tell me her marriage is in trouble.'

'I wouldn't exactly say that it's in trouble...' Harriet started, but her voice trailed off as she conceded the point. 'OK, it's in big trouble.'

'I'm sorry,' Ciro responded politely. 'But at least it means that we can rule out an ectopic! Now...' Sensing her need to change the subject, he stood up and adopted a rather more professional distance. 'Which means we have to consider that you could have appendicitis.'

'No.'

'Are you going to tell me that your appendix and you haven't been getting on for a while, that it's been treating itself to massages while you weren't looking? That it's been so neglected there isn't any chance it could be inflamed?'

A tiny smile wobbled on her pale lips.

'I'll need to examine you properly, Harriet, there's absolutely nothing to be embarrassed about.'

There was *everything* to be embarrassed about. He could be as matter-of-fact as he liked, pull on a pair of gloves as casually as if he were about to do the dishes, but there was no way, *no way*, she was going to let Ciro Delgato examine her *there*. She'd never in a million years be able to work with him if she allowed him to. Quite simply, she'd have to resign.

'I'll go to my own GP tomorrow,' Harriet begged, desperate suddenly for the lyrical sound of her lovely GP's voice as she chatted about her children and grandchildren, a GP who somehow made even the most uncomfortable procedures as routine as a gossip at the supermarket checkout—not like this Spanish dynamo that she'd have to work with again.

'What is it about me that all my patients wish to suddenly leave and see their own GPs in the morning?'

'It isn't you,' Harriet lied. 'It's just…' She struggled for an explanation. 'I want to go home, Ciro, to my own bed. If this had happened at home I wouldn't have even come into hospital.'

'What if I call down one of the surgeons to examine you, see if there's a female doctor on?'

'I just want to go home. Drew will be there. If I get worse, he'll bring me straight back.'

'I thought you said—'

'We're having some problems, Ciro, but he's not going to leave me rolling around in agony, it's not that bad!'

He stared at her thoughtfully for a long moment and just when she thought he was about to read the Riot Act, amazingly he conceded—albeit reluctantly.

'If it worsens, you are to come straight back to the hospital.'

'I will.'

'And even if you feel better, you are to see your GP first thing in the morning.'

'Yes.'

'Can I at least take some blood and I'll fax the results over to your GP? You can give me his name.'

'Her name,' Harriet needlessly corrected. 'And yes.' She'd have agreed to anything just to get the hell out of there.

'Would you like me to call your husband to come and fetch you?'

'No,' Harriet answered immediately, imagining Drew's mood if she dragged him out of bed at one a.m. because of a stomach pain when he had a photo shoot in the morning.

'You're not driving yourself home.'

'Then I'll take a taxi,' Harriet responded, with absolutely no intention of doing so, given she felt so much better.

'OK, I'll draw some blood and leave you to get dressed.'

But any thoughts of dashing to the car park were soon laid to rest when Ciro insisted on walking her to the taxi rank outside Emergency and ensuring she was safely in a taxi, even reminding her, as if she were a child, to put her seat belt on.

'Do you escort all your patients to their vehicles?' Harriet bristled.

'Only if I believe they'd be stupid enough to ignore my instructions. If you get any worse, you're—'

'To come straight back. I know, I know.'

As the taxi pulled off, despite her reddened eyes and nose, despite the pain in her stomach and the appalling mess of her marriage, Harriet felt a feeling so unfamiliar it took a second or two to register what it was.

Peace.

A tiny corner of peace in her soul.

Finally she'd told someone, finally she'd admitted the truth, and the world hadn't stopped turning. In fact, the world had carried happily on. Ciro hadn't stared at her, utterly appalled. Instead, he'd told her a simple truth.

She wasn't alone.

The world might be happily turning but she wasn't the only one facing this type of problem and somehow it comforted her, somehow it gave her strength.

Paying the taxi driver, Harriet rummaged in her bag for her keys, turning them slowly in the lock and trying to creep in the front door without waking Drew, only this time it wasn't because she was afraid of confrontation but because, quite simply, she wasn't up to dealing with it right now. But when this was over, when her stomach was better, she was going to sit down with Drew and talk, really talk for once, find out where their marriage was exactly, and where, if anywhere, it was going. It was time to face the truth.

Literally!

* * *

Seeing them lying together, Harriet witnessed at first hand the passion that had been missing in this bed for so long now, that long blonde hair tumbling over the pillowcase, her pillowcase, the one that she, Harriet, had washed, ironed and put on! Facing a fact more appalling than any she had considered, for the second time that night, Harriet choked back bile, only a grumbling appendix had nothing to do with it.

'Harriet!'

Shocked eyes, which she'd thought she'd known, snapped open as she turned on the light, her own eyes widening in disgusted horror as the blonde, thin beauty beside him uncoiled her tanned long limbs and taking in the scene had the gall to smirk somewhat defiantly over at Harriet.

'Please, don't try and tell me that it's not what I think.' Furious, embarrassed, Harriet turned and ran, taking the steps two at a time, shaking Drew off when he caught up with her, a hastily wrapped towel around his waist.

'Harriet, please, don't just walk out. We need to talk.'

'Talk to me through your solicitor, Drew.' She shook her head as if to clear it. 'That's why you were nice to me tonight. All that crap about getting me a hot-water bottle, pretending that you care, when all the time you were just glad I was going to work so your tart—'

'Harriet, don't be like that.'

'What is she, then? What *lady* would get into someone else's marital bed while the wife was out working? My God, Drew, I've worked my backside off to put you through acting school, put up with all your moods and insecurities when all you could get was a couple of walk-on parts, even upped and moved yet again, so you could take this job. And this is how you treat me. Don't expect nice here, Drew, don't expect me to smile and say it's OK, as I have done over the years when you treat me like dirt…'

'You need to calm down,' he said. 'We need to work out what we're going to do—'

'You mean we need to work out what we're going to tell people?' Harriet retorted bitterly. 'Why? Are you worried that if the press find out that your new agent mightn't be pleased, worried that your popularity ratings might dip for a week or two? That's it, isn't it? You don't give a damn what this is doing to me, all you're worried about is how it's going to affect you! All those nights I've been working for us!'

'You've been working because you love your job,' Drew sneered.

'Not that much, Drew!' Harriet retorted. 'Not sixty-hour weeks just so that you can pursue your dreams. The difference between you and I is that I didn't constantly moan about it, didn't assume the world was against me because I had to earn a living the hard way.'

'Hard!' Drew blazed. 'Have you any idea what my work involves? The constant demands, the pressure to always look the part. All you have to do is pull on a uniform…'

On and on, the same old song she had danced to over the years, only this time it was a different tune. This time Harriet didn't automatically back down, because the reason she was home at two in the morning was making itself known, the misery that had brought her to this moment was repeating itself, only this time when nausea struck she didn't make a blind dash for the bathroom—she knew that there was no one to guide her, and it should have been mortifying, should have been the indignity to top them all, but seeing the horror in

Drew's eyes as she threw up on the smart cream carpet made her, for some inexplicable reason, want to laugh.

'So my job's easy, is it?' Her defiant eyes met his. 'Well, see how much you enjoy cleaning up someone else's mess.'

The cool night air on her flaming cheeks as she burst out the front door slapped some sense into her. Harriet knew she should go back, knew she should demand that the other woman leave her home—Drew, too, for that matter—but lousy at confrontation at the best of times, all she wanted now was to be alone. She made her way to the bus shelter at the end of her street and sat for how long she didn't know, staring at the tiny sliver of a new moon, eyes curiously dry as she gazed up to the skies. And at that moment she knew without reservation that her marriage was over, that, no matter what, there would be no going back.

Now what?

She didn't know if she said it out loud, acutely aware now of the precariousness of her situation. Obviously unwell, she should be in bed, but there was no way she was going back there.

A hotel perhaps? Making to stand, she gave in even before the thought had formed—a searing pain forcing her back to the cold wooden bench.

Clutching her stomach, Harriet consoled herself that it had been a stupid idea anyway. How the hell was she supposed to get to a hotel when her car was back at Emergency and her keys were back at the house, along with her mobile phone, when all she had on her was a couple of coins for the Emergency vending machine and an ID badge hanging around her neck.

'What am I going to do?'

This time she did say it out loud, teeth chattering as she clutched at her stomach, hating with a passion her appendix, which had chosen this time in her life to introduce itself to its owner. The bright lights of the phone booth across the road beckoned her to come over.

And it was the longest, loneliest walk of her life, the most difficult call she had ever made, picking up a telephone and dialling the emergency number, listening to the calm voice at the other end as she tried to fashion her mounting hysteria into a voice, to say the three little words that no one ever really wanted to say.

'I need help!'

CHAPTER FOUR

EVEN though it was the last thing she wanted to happen, the sound of the sirens in the distance were a welcome relief. The pain in Harriet's stomach was so severe now she couldn't even sit. All she could do was lie on the bench as the ambulance pulled up and the familiar faces of Max and Tara appeared, their green jumpsuits as familiar as her own nursing uniform, their tender professionalism everything she needed as they gently asked her what had happened.

'I was unwell at work. The doctor thought I might have appendicitis…'

'He let you go home?' Tara asked, surprised, then gave a low laugh. 'Or did Sister Farrell insist that she knew better?'

'Something like that. I'm so sorry to drag you guys out. Maybe I should have called a taxi.'

'Don't be daft.' Max shook his head as he dragged the stretcher from the ambulance to the bus stop, having realised at a glance there was no way she could make the short walk to the ambulance. 'We'll get you in the warm vehicle and get a drip started. Here, have a few sucks on this before we move you.'

A plastic tube was handed to her and Harriet dragged

on it, grateful for the short relief the painkiller offered as they slowly lifted her onto the stretcher and moved her into the ambulance.

'Do we have to go local?' Harriet asked, knowing the answer before it came.

'It's an emergency callout,' Tara responded, concentrating on inserting the drip into Harriet's hand. 'We have to take you to the nearest hospital and, given that you've already been seen there by a doctor tonight, surely it makes sense…' Seeing Harriet's eyes fill with embarrassed tears, she changed track. 'Your friends are there, Harriet, people who know and care about you. They'll give you the five-star treatment. Surely that can only be good?'

But she didn't want the five-star treatment. Instead, she wanted unknown faces treating an unknown patient, couldn't bear the thought of having to answer the question that would surely be on everyone's lips.

'What were you doing at a bus stop?'

Over and over the question had been asked—by the paramedics, by Louise, who was still stuck on Triage, by the nursing supervisor as she'd directed the stretcher into cubicle one in an attempt to spare Harriet the indignity of the entire department seeing her brought in, by Susan, her concerned face looming over her as she pumped up the blood-pressure cuff. 'You were supposed to be at home. Why on earth didn't you just—?'

'Enough!'

The single word, however sharply spoken, couldn't disguise the thick accent, and as the staff finally melted away, Harriet closed her eyes in shame as Ciro stood over her. He'd already examined her on arrival and commenced treatment, but thankfully that was a distant vague blur, but now the fluids that were being delivered intravenously were starting to kick in and the oxygen being administered through nasal prongs was having the supposed desired effect, the world was starting to come back into focus. Harriet listened as he dismissed the gathered nurses and paramedics, waiting until the cubicle was vacant before finally she managed to peel her eyes open, bracing herself for the question she had heard incessantly since her arrival.

Instead, it was answered.

'Your husband is staying in a hotel for work, and had you told me that you knew I wouldn't have let you go home alone…'

Confused, Harriet blinked back at him.

'You've had trouble with the phone since you moved in, haven't you?'

'Thank you.' It was all she could manage, her voice strangling in her throat as Ciro dealt with the social absurdities that still mattered at times like this. 'I just couldn't bear everyone's sympathy at the moment, the gossip that would start. I'm just so ashamed.'

'Silly girl,' Ciro said, but not unkindly, the backs of his fingers sweeping her forehead to check her temperature. 'You should—'

'Should have what, Ciro?' Harriet interrupted. 'I found my husband in bed with another woman. I was hardly going to ask them to move over so that I could lie down! What did you expect me to do?'

'I don't know,' he admitted. 'I'm just glad that you had the presence of mind to call for help when you did. Had you not called, your appendix might have ruptured and you would have been very ill indeed.'

'It was either call for help or sit at the bus stop all night.'

'Life will start to look up very soon.'

'It has to.' Sunken, dry eyes stared back at him. 'After all, just how low can one person go?'

'You should be asking Drew that, Harriet, not yourself.'

'How did you know?' she gulped. 'I mean, how did you guess what had happened when I went home?'

He gave a vague shrug. 'You said yourself that nothing was happening in the…' His English wasn't that good, but painfully she caught the drift. 'It was stupid of me to send you home unannounced in the early hours of the the morning, given what you'd told me. I'm sorry,' he added, as if this whole stupid mess was his fault. 'It must have been awful for you.'

'I was sick on the carpet.' Why she was filling him in, Harriet had no idea, but somehow sharing the most embarrassing details made them seem less so. 'I left it for him to clean up—told him that if he thought my job was so easy then he should try it.'

'Good for you.' A smile broke out on his face and even though she'd seen him smile before it was like witnessing it for the first time because now it was aimed entirely at her—his eyes softer now, intimate almost. Not for the first time that night, Harriet felt bewildered and confused, but for entirely different reasons.

Impossibly shy all of a sudden, she lowered her eyes. 'Can I have some Maxalon now?'

'You already have.' He attempted a smile. 'And a massive dose of pethidine. That's why you're able to talk. The surgeon is ready for you in Theatre. You'll go to EHU afterwards. Unfortunately there aren't any beds on the surgical ward, but I'm sure they'll find you a side room tomorrow.'

EHU stood for Emergency Holding Unit, a rapid-turnover ward that acted as a holding bay for emergency patients when the wards were full, but Harriet couldn't have cared less where she was admitted. At least she'd have a bed for a couple of days! All she wanted right now was for the pain in her stomach to go so she could focus on the pain in her heart.

'Is there anyone you want me to call for you?' Ciro asked, ever practical.

Harriet shook her head.

'What about your parents?'

'There's only Mum, she lives in Perth.' It was all she could manage, her lips almost numb, her mind curiously clear. 'I don't want to worry her.'

'What about your husband?' Ciro pressed gently. 'He is your next of kin. Someone ought to know what's happening to you.'

'Please, don't call him.' She shook her head against the pillow. 'I just don't want to see him yet.'

'OK,' Ciro soothed. 'I'm not going to do anything without your permission. But perhaps this may be the wake-up call he needs—'

'It's over,' Harriet broke in, her voice the firmest it had been since her arrival in the department, her mind completely made up. 'I'm just not up to telling the world yet. Oh, hell, Ciro, what am I—?'

'Shh…' His hand was back on her forehead, only this time he wasn't checking her temperature. This time he was brushing back a couple of strands of hair, soothing her, pushing her back down to the foggy oblivion the pethidine afforded, that gorgeous full mouth, softly speaking, telling her that it would all be OK, that all she had to do was concentrate on getting well, to close her eyes and just go to sleep.

But she didn't want to.

Didn't want to close her eyes on the sweetest pain-killer of them all.

CHAPTER FIVE

'HARRIET?'

A million adolescents would have given their entire year's pocket money to wake up to that face, but when Harriet opened her eyes all she wanted was to close them again. She'd been back from Theatre a few hours now, but had slept for the most part, vaguely acknowledging the absurdity that Alyssa, who she had cared for the previous night, now lay in the next bed to her. The world was way too confusing to face right now, but any chance of a longer reprieve from her problems faded as Drew's face came into unwelcome view. Everything about him revolted her now—the blond hair he faithfully had streaked to capture the surfie look, the spray-on tan that was carefully shaded to accentuate his gym-toned muscles. Squinting to focus, Harriet stared at the man who had caused her so much pain, the previous night's events pinging in with alarming clarity. She watched as he braced himself for her stinging words, but instead of accusations she said the first thing that sprang to her anaesthetic-riddled mind, with no offence meant, but not caring if it were taken.

'You pluck your eyebrows.'

Irritated, he shook his head as he stood up and pulled

the curtains around her, clearly not wanting the scene made public. 'Don't be daft.'

'You do.' Running a dry tongue over even drier lips, she stared at two perfectly formed arches. 'They look nothing like they did when we were first married. Can you open the curtains, please?'

'Let's just keep them closed, can we? The kid in the next bed has been hounding me for my autograph.'

'And did you give it to her?'

'I came here to see you, Harriet, not make small talk with some kid.'

With one hand holding her tender stomach, she reached to the table over her bed, declining his out-stretched hand and choosing to get the small cup of water herself.

'The nurse said you should just have a small sip,' Drew admonished, making to take the cup from her, but Harriet gripped it tightly.

'And we all know the respect you have for nurses.' Defiantly she took another long sip before placing the cup back on the table and gingerly lying back down.

'How did you know I was here?' she finally asked, disappointed that Ciro had broken her confidence, yet understanding why he might have thought he had to.

'I got a call on my mobile, someone called Susan. She thought I was staying in some hotel or some-thing…' He tried to take her hand but she pulled it away. 'From the way she was talking I gather that you didn't tell them what had happened.'

'Do you blame me?'

'I'm sorry, Harriet.'

He even looked it, tears glistening in his eyes, running a worried hand through his tousled hair, but, she reminded herself firmly, Drew was an actor, able to cry on demand, able to play the part of guilt-ridden spouse to a T if last week's episodes of his show were anything to go by.

'Are you sorry that you got caught, Drew, or sorry that it's over?' When he didn't speak, she did it for him, asked what she needed to know. 'How long has it been going on, Drew? How long have you been seeing her?'

'It meant nothing,' he offered, clearly confused when she blinked at him in disbelief.

'And that's supposed to make me feel better? You don't get it, do you? You don't understand that the fact she meant nothing just cheapens our marriage even more.'

'Please, Harriet, if you'll just let me speak—'

'I meant what I said last night, Drew. You can speak to me through my solicitor.'

'You don't have a solicitor,' Drew pointed out. 'Look, we have to work out what we're going to say. You might not think it matters, but when this gets out it's going to affect us both. Harriet!' he pleaded when she shrugged her shoulders. 'You couldn't bring yourself to tell your colleagues, so do you really want them reading about it in the newspaper?'

'I guess,' Harriet sighed, 'we'll just say it was amicable, no hard feelings on either side. And if we're going to lie, why not add that there was no one else involved?'

'When will you get out?'

'Tomorrow probably.'

'So soon.' He gave a small look of alarm. 'I'll move into the spare bedroom…'

'There's no point, Drew, I'm not coming home. I can't go back there, not after what happened.'

'Do you want me to move out?'

It was the first decent thing he'd done in the whole debacle but, staring up at the ceiling, Harriet shook her head.

'But where will you go? Who's going to take care of you?'

It was a good question, one she had been asking herself since she'd first come to, but even if her bravado was false, even if she was terrified of what lay ahead, she damn well wasn't going to let him see that. Pale blue eyes were proud and defiant as she turned her head to face him.

'That's no longer your concern, Drew.'

'Is there anything you want me to do?'

'Pack me a case.' Swallowing hard, determined not to cry in front of him, she struggled to keep her voice even. 'Just drop it off at the nurses' station.'

'Anything else?' And maybe he wasn't acting now, because his nose was actually running and there were tears in his eyes as maybe, somewhere deep inside, the ramifications hit home, that the Harriet he had known for so long now could never, ever forgive this. 'Is there anything else you want?'

'Nothing.' She turned her face away, feeling a tear slide down the side of her face and into the pillow as an unwitting nurse swished open the curtain and Drew walked away. Harriet couldn't really believe how much her life had changed in a few short hours, that after all this time her marriage really was over.

And as superficial and selfish as he could be at times, Drew wasn't a complete bastard. Underneath all his hype there was still a glimmer of the man she had married, the man she had once loved. As he walked out Harriet heard Alyssa's breathless voice call his name, listened with a pensive tiny smile as, even though he must be hurting too, he did the decent thing in the end— he stopped for a short chat.

Made another girl's day.

* * *

'Please, don't tell me that I'm better off without him.' Putting her hand over her face, trying to hold it all in, she didn't even have the emotional strength to be embarrassed when Ciro walked in to check on the patients he had admitted overnight before finally heading home. The last thing she needed was a few empty platitudes. 'Because I know that I am. I know it's been over for ages. It's just…'

'Hard?' Ciro offered, and Harriet nodded from behind her hand.

'It gets better, I promise.'

'How would you know?' It wasn't a particularly gracious response but she was past caring.

'Because I've been there, very recently actually.'

Fingers parting, she peered out at him.

'Were you married?'

'No.'

'Did you have surgery the night you found your partner in bed with someone else?'

'No.'

'Were your family on the other side of the country?'

'No.' He gave a soft laugh. 'I've no idea what you're going through, have I? I'll shut up now.'

She gave a thin smile.

'How you are you feeling?'

'It's painful, of course, but not as much as I expected it to be.'

'I wasn't speaking as your doctor, I was asking how *you* were feeling.'

Pale eyes squinted up at him. 'As I said, it's painful, of course, but not as much as I expected it to be.'

'I'm sorry.'

'You don't have to be.'

'Is there anything that you need?'

Harriet shook her head. 'Drew's going to pack a case for me.' She registered his frown. 'He offered to move out, but I told him I don't want to go back there. I'll go and sort out my things when I'm more up to it.'

'So what will you do now? Where will you go?'

'I'll be fine,' Harriet said with rather more confidence than she felt. She wanted him to just go, couldn't bear to see the sympathy in his eyes. 'Could you pull the curtains as you leave?'

And maybe some of it had been lost in translation, because Ciro did pull the curtains, but remained beside her bed, staring down at her for a while before finally talking.

'Harriet, what will you do when you are discharged? I mean, who will look after you? Are you going to stay with a friend?'

Why wouldn't he just leave it, why did he have to just keep pushing, making her feel like some sort of social misfit? It wasn't as if she didn't have friends, but, given the fact she'd only been in Sydney six months, they were hardly close enough to ask if she could borrow their spare room to recuperate. But instead of explaining, Harriet gave a tight shrug.

'What about Judith?'

'Judith?' Harriet gave a slightly incredulous laugh.

'She speaks very highly of you.'

'Since when were you and Judith on speaking terms?'

'I telephoned her last night about an hour after she went off duty.' Ciro shrugged. 'Our altercation left me with an aftertaste.' Harriet didn't even attempt to correct him, his poor English didn't matter. That he had taken the time to call Judith and set the record straight, even though she had treated him so rudely, had her blinking in awe at his insight. 'She said that you had already spoken to her and she was feeling much better.' He gave a tight smile. 'We both apologised.'

'She's as soft as butter really.' Harriet smiled fondly.

'And she was most concerned about you when she arrived on duty.'

'I'm not asking Judith if I can stay with her,' Harriet responded firmly. 'I'll check into a motel or something.'

'Look,' he said, as if it were open for discussion, as if she'd actually asked for his help, 'I'm staying in serviced apartments. They're very nice, right on the beach, there's a gym, a pool.'

'I'm recovering from an operation,' Harriet snapped. 'I'm hardly up for an aerobic workout.'

'The rooms are serviced daily, the beds made, the dishes done—at least you could concentrate on yourself. Why don't you think about it? It really is a good idea.'

'I know why you're doing this.' Her blue eyes flashed, embarrassment making her angry. 'Just because you're the only one who knows what's going on with my life, it doesn't mean you have to step in. I'm not asking for help.'

'And that is what is so annoying!' Ciro retorted, his response equally sharp. 'Why you have to make this an issue? And I know,' he added before Harriet could, 'that I said that terribly, but don't correct me to avoid the issue.'

'I'm not avoiding anything.' Harriet sniffed.

'Oh, yes, you are,' Ciro responded. 'You're so damned independent, so damned used to coping with things by yourself, you can't bear the thought of leaning on someone.'

Independent! Never in a million years would Harriet have used that word to describe herself. She was stunned that that was how Ciro perceived her. Up till then she'd assumed he was feeling sorry for her.

It came as a pleasant surprise to realise that she actually infuriated him.

'Look, Ciro, we barely know each other. We've only worked together for half a night, it's hardly enough to become flatmates!'

She'd never heard him laugh before, a deep, low laugh, and if she'd been embarrassed before, when he spoke next, Harriet was mortified.

'Hardly. But I happen to know that the apartment on the floor below me has just become vacant.'

'Oh.'

'I could speak to the landlord for you.'

'Oh.'

'Would you like me to?'

When she didn't answer, Ciro pushed a touch harder. 'The rates are quite reasonable.' Harriet's eyes widened as he told her the weekly rental. Clearly, Ciro's vision of reasonable differed from hers, but the thought of having the bed made and the vacuuming done, of bay views and gentle walks along the beach while she got her head together were starting to make themselves known. Fiercely expensive it may be, but over the years she'd been so boringly good with money, she'd somehow managed to support Drew *and* put a bit away for a rainy day.

Well, the rainy day had arrived and it was pouring.

Pouring.

Force-ten gales were howling, sandbags were out and it was time to strap on her buoyancy jacket—time to do as the emergency cards on planes said and look after herself first for once and stop worrying about everyone else.

'There's also a restaurant on the ground floor. They offer room service.'

'Sold!' Harriet said finally.

'Sold?' Ciro questioned.

'That's a yes, Ciro.' She smiled. 'Yes, please. It would be great if you could ask the landlord.'

'I'll come and see you tonight before the shift starts, hopefully with a set of keys!'

'I haven't got my bag,' Harriet said. 'Drew should be bringing it later today. I can write a cheque for the bond then.'

'No worries.' Ciro gave her a surprised look. 'I'm starting to sound like an Aussie!'

'No, Ciro, you're not.' Harriet grinned, and her smile stayed as he walked away from her bedside and stopped to talk with Alyssa, stayed as she lay on the bed, staring at the ceiling, and stayed despite the fact that this should be the worst day of her life.

There was absolutely no chance of dying quietly on EHU, no chance to lie in bed and lick her wounds. Instead, after her obs had been checked yet again and her drip was taken down and a post-op wash given, Harriet was walked the length of the unit by an eager, chirpy physio. She gingerly put one foot in front of the other and held onto her wound as the blessed woman reminded her incessantly to take deep breaths and to remember to wiggle her toes while in bed. Harriet caught Alyssa's eye as she walked past. Declining the cheery suggestion to 'pop back into bed', Harriet chose instead to perch on Alyssa's just as lunch was being served.

'What happened to you?' Alyssa asked, putting down the magazine Drew had signed. 'I thought it was you when they wheeled you back from Theatre, but I couldn't be sure. I mean, you never really imagine the nurses getting sick.'

'I had my appendix out.' Harriet smiled, but it changed midway as she winced slightly as she sat on the bed. 'I'll be fine in a couple of days. How are you doing?'

'They're admitting me to a medical ward this afternoon.' Alyssa screwed up her nose. 'They've put this horrible tube down my nose into my stomach and if I don't eat my meals they're going to feed me some disgusting supplement. I want to pull it out.'

'It's just a short-term thing,' Harriet said softly, pleasantly surprised that Alyssa had even agreed to it.

'That's what Dr Delgato said.' Alyssa sniffed, leaning back on the mountain of pillows supporting her tiny frame. 'I wish it was him looking after me, not the stupid old fuddy-duddy that came and saw me this morning. He told me off for not eating my breakfast, he said that if I wanted to get better then I had to start eating, but it's just so hard.'

'I know,' Harriet sympathised, wincing at the doctor's insensitivity, knowing that for Alyssa it just wasn't that simple.

'Dr Delgato said that once I'm a bit stronger they're going to admit me to the adolescent unit.' Harriet heard the tremor of fear in the young girl's voice, but any chance of comforting her was snatched away when a nurse deposited a large meal tray on her table.

'Lunch, Alyssa,' the nurse said firmly, removing the lid from the tray and pouring out a large glass of milk. 'I want to see that all gone by the time I get back.'

And she meant well, Harriet didn't doubt it, but it was just way, way too soon to even be talking to Alyssa like that. Seeing the sparkle of tears in the young girl's eyes, Harriet watched as Alyssa pushed the peas around her plate, dug her fork into the mashed potato, stabbed at the fish dripping in butter sauce, not once lifting the fork to her mouth. 'He said he'd come and see me on the adolescent unit to see how I was doing.'

'Who?'

'Dr Delgato,' Alyssa said, and Harriet was hard pushed to keep the frown from her face. It was very easy to make promises, to tell a teary, scared patient when you were trying to placate them that you would be there for them, but it was another thing to see them through. In this case the damage that could be done if Ciro didn't follow through could be very detrimental—trust was a very important factor with this type of patient. 'He said that he'd come and see how I was getting on, that I just had to grin and bear it while I was on the medical ward, and that once they transferred me to the adolescent unit it would be better, that I'd be among people who understood. I know that I'm going to be here for ages. The doctor on this morning told me to forget about the concert.'

'You're not well enough to dance at the moment.'

'I know,' Alyssa admitted. 'It's not just the concert, though. If I'd danced well there was a good chance I'd have been given a scholarship...' Her tiny voice wobbled. Her eyes screwed closed, Alyssa went on bravely, 'Mum's going to be so disappointed.'

There was nothing Harriet could say without crossing the line. In a single sentence Alyssa had summed up the complexity of her problems, the pressures, real or imagined, that had brought her to this point, the complex dynamics that fed this insidious disease. And there was so much Harriet wanted to say, so much she wanted to do. She wanted to delve deeper, to help unravel the complex puzzle, to untangle the knots that clouded Alyssa's fragile mind, but a half-hour gossip on the edge of her bed wouldn't suffice. Alyssa didn't need an emergency nurse with empathy, she needed skilled specialist care, and Harriet knew that she must not complicate matters, must not, no matter how much she might want to, say anything that might jeopardise Alyssa's treatment.

Knew that she wasn't qualified to help.

'Oh, come on, Alyssa.' The nurse was back, frowning down at the plate. 'You haven't even tried. You know what this means, don't you?'

And Harriet had to bite her tongue, knew it wasn't her place to argue, so instead she took the tiny frail hand in hers as the plate was finally removed, stroked the translucent skin as the nurse set up the kangaroo pump, attaching a large bag of supplement to Alyssa's NG tube and setting the dose before walking away. Harriet watched as with every whir of the motor a tear slid down Alyssa's fragile cheeks, knowing, if not understanding, the torture Alyssa felt was being inflicted on her.

'Dr Delgato's right,' Harriet said finally, gently squeezing Alyssa's hand. 'Once you're moved to the adolescent unit you'll be in the right place, you'll be getting the help you need. Things will sort themselves out.'

'Will they?'

Terrified eyes held Harriet's and even if she wasn't entirely qualified to answer, surely common sense could prevail.

'With a bit of give and take,' she responded finally. 'From both sides.'

CHAPTER SIX

'HOPEFULLY this is adequate.'

Turning the key in the door, Ciro pushed it open and stood aside as Harriet gingerly stepped inside her new home.

Ciro had duly picked her up from the surgical ward as arranged when his shift had ended. Harriet had rolled her eyes at the raised eyebrows from more than a few of her colleagues as Ciro had waited patiently for her to be given her discharge letter and say goodbye to the nurses that had treated her.

Drew had barely tried and had spectacularly failed yet again. He had packed a pair of white linen shorts Harriet had been *hoping* to slim into and a lilac halter neck that was definitely meant for days when one was feeling good about themselves, as opposed to the day you were being discharged from hospital, not to mention the trendy espadrilles that needed slender legs—and those were the wearable bits! A fluorescent pink bikini and a pair of jeans more suited to Alyssa were a couple of other choice items Drew had thought-lessly tossed in, but at least finally she had her handbag and purse back.

Declining Ciro's suggestion of a wheelchair, she had

instead limped along a corridor that she normally raced down, acutely aware of her pale legs that shouldn't be seen in white shorts and her straight red hair that had suffered some sort of major collapse under the hospital's version of shampoo. By the time she'd reached Ciro's very impressive, very new black car Harriet had been more than ready to sink into the cream leather and close her eyes for the journey ahead.

Until he climbed into the driver's seat.

Until the scent that had reached her nostrils on their one and only shift together had assailed her again. Until his hand had brushed her bare leg as he'd let out the handbrake.

Out of the relatively safe confines of the hospital, stripped bare of the safety of her uniform, suddenly she had felt exposed and vulnerable and she'd spent the entire journey in a state of nervousness, trying and failing to make small talk. But as they'd driven along the beach road, Ciro had gestured to the apartments set high and proud on a large rock that jutted into the ocean and Harriet's breath had caught in her throat. She had scarcely been able to believe this was going to be her home for the foreseeable future.

Adequate didn't come close to describing the massive, sun-drenched apartment that greeted her tired eyes, everything in the huge lounge geared towards the floor-to-ceiling windows that took in the endlessly divine sight of the Pacific Ocean. Waves eternally rolled in, the roar silenced by the closed doors. But, as everyone who stepped in surely must, Harriet walked straight across the polished jarrah floorboards to the balcony, hardly noticing the tasteful occasional furniture. She flicked open the catch, slid the windows open and stepped out onto the huge balcony. In a clever architectural feat, instead of facing out onto the ocean, the architect had angled the building, and as Harriet stepped out onto the balcony she could see exactly why—whichever way she turned the views were divine. Facing outwards, she could see the length of the beach, watch the joggers pounding along, yet if she turned around it was as if she were sitting adrift in the water, watching the pounding waves roll in towards her.

'It's divine,' Harriet breathed. 'It's the most amazing view!'

'I haven't turned on my television since I moved in,' Ciro admitted. 'I'll just go and get your case from the car.'

'Thank you.' Harriet smiled and as Ciro went to go she said it again. 'I really mean that, Ciro. Thank you so much for doing all this for me.'

'It really is no big deal,' Ciro said modestly. 'I knew that the apartment was vacant and that you needed somewhere to live. Of course, I may live to regret it.' He smiled at her frown. 'You might revel so much in your new-found freedom that you take to throwing wild parties every night.' He pointed to the ceiling. 'I'm in the apartment above you.'

'I doubt that I'll be throwing too many wild parties, at least not on week nights,' Harriet said.

Suddenly the amazing view dimmed a notch. Turning to face him, Harriet had to squint to bring his features into focus, the harsh morning sun behind him rendering his features unreadable as she voiced an apology that had bubbled for a couple of days now.

'I was very dismissive of you in the hospital.'

'Dismissive?'

'When you told me you'd just come out of a relationship,' Harriet explained. 'I was feeling incredibly sorry for myself and to imply that you couldn't possibly understand what I was going through just because you weren't married…'

'And didn't have surgery that day!' Ciro teased. 'Or find my lover in bed with someone else!'

'You were trying to be nice and I was very rude, and for that I'm sorry.'

'Forget it,' Ciro said easily.

Only Harriet couldn't.

Suddenly the details that she had waved away mattered now. Suddenly, for reasons she didn't even want to fathom, Harriet wanted to know about Ciro's past, wanted to know if there was someone in his present…

'You said it hurt,' Harriet pushed, hoping she could blame her rise in colour on the fierce sun. 'What happened?'

'That's the sort of question that can only be answered over a very large glass of wine,' Ciro responded, smiling, but something in his voice told her she'd crossed a line, that that subject was closed, and he confirmed it when, without pausing for breath, he headed back inside. 'I'll go and get your case.'

Oh, hell!

Groaning with mortification, Harriet waited for her front door to close safely before she headed back inside, her eyes barely registering her new surroundings. Instead, she sat down on a navy leather sofa and buried her burning cheeks in her hands.

'What happened?' Harriet mimicked her own voice a couple of times, wincing as she did so. What did it matter to her what had happened in Ciro's past? What business was it of hers to ask him about his relationships? It must have sounded as if she fancied him or something.

Which was ridiculous.

Ridiculous, Harriet affirmed. She had just been making conversation. As if she was even remotely interested in a relationship at the moment. Her marriage had only just ended, she'd just had surgery, she was here to recuperate, to get over the hellish past few days and gather her strength for the undoubted battles that lay ahead. So what if Ciro was good-looking, so what if he'd been kind, so what if he was the only person on earth who she'd trusted with her predicament...?

'Are you OK?' Depositing her suitcase on the lounge floor, he made his way straight over to her, clearly mistaking her hunched position on the sofa and groans as some kind of relapse. 'What happened?'

'Nothing,' Harriet started, then decided that surely she could be excused a tiny white lie. 'Actually, I just came over a bit dizzy. I'll be fine in a moment.'

'Bed!' Ciro declared, guiding her up by the elbow and practically frogmarching her towards the bedroom. Under any other circumstances it would have been a dream come true! 'No arguments!'

He didn't get one.

Mute, she stood there as he pulled the wooden slats on the divine view then proceeded to pull back starched white sheets. Her lies caught up with her as she truly did start to feel dizzy, only it had nothing to do with standing up too quickly and everything to do with the man guiding her by the elbow to the bedside and gently lifting her legs onto the bed.

'Bed for me, too,' Ciro said. 'I've done my penance on nights.'

'I like nights,' Harriet admitted.

'Me, too. Especially when you start in a new job. It forces you to find out where things are and how the system works. Right…' He'd tucked her in firmly, the sheet well past her neck. 'If you need anything…'

'I won't.' Harriet shook her head, determined to redeem herself, to show she wanted nothing more from him than a courteous professional relationship and a friendly nod of greeting if they met on the stairs.

But it was Ciro lingering now, Ciro prolonging the conversation.

'How long till you go back to work?'

'They gave me two weeks.'

'Well, use it wisely.'

She nodded, holding her breath, wishing he would go, yet somehow wanting him to stay a bit longer. He was just so easy to talk to, his smile, his demeanour so very disarming, Ciro Delgato did without trying something no man had ever done before. His mere presence soothed her, yet simultaneously excited her. She had a need to get to know him deeper, to find out what had brought him here, how long he was staying. But it was none of her business, Harriet reminded herself firmly. He had done her a huge favour in finding her this divine apartment—the last thing he needed in return was a nosy neighbour with a king-sized crush.

The internal admission shocked her, and as she lay stock-still her mind whirred.

It was a crush—a stupid crush—and all because he had helped her at her very worst, made her laugh when she should have cried, taken the pressure off the practicalities of finding somewhere to live and dealing with inquisitive colleagues.

'You have to take things easy.' Ciro's voice was insistent. 'Not so long ago people stayed in hospital for a full week after having their appendix removed. I really don't like the thought of you having no one to take care of you.'

'Ciro, I don't need anyone to take care of me. I'm fine by myself.'

'That sounds like the title of a song.'

'It's just how I feel.' Harriet shrugged. 'I really would prefer to be on my own right now. Mum and my friends all mean well, but I'm just—'

'Fair enough,' he broke in softly. 'Can I drop by and check on you? I won't impose,' he added quickly before she could shake her head. 'I'd just feel better if I saw that you were OK.'

Which was OK to agree to, Harriet decided. After all, she'd do the same for a neighbour. Giving a small nod, she closed her eyes, fully expecting to hear the bedroom door close, to be left alone with her jumbled thoughts. But he stayed.

'When you're up to it…'

Her eyes opened to his voice. She turned her head on the pillow to face him, and even though the light was dim it accentuated somehow how tired he must be, the hollows of his cheekbones deepened, that five a.m. shadow that was positively charcoal now. 'We'll have that talk.'

'Talk?' Harriet croaked, grateful that he had closed the slats and couldn't see her flaming cheeks, anticipation flaring in every heightened nerve, simultaneously berating herself at her own presumption.

'Over that large glass of wine. I'd like to get to know you better, Harriet.' She didn't answer, couldn't. Her eyes wide, she blinked at him, though his expression was impossible to read in the semi-darkness. 'Rest now,' he said, his voice thick and heavily accented, the door closing softly behind him.

In the days that followed Harriet truly wasn't sure if she'd dreamt the last part of the conversation, if her drug-

and anaesthetic-hazed mind had somehow played tricks on her, because surely there hadn't been that hint of promise throbbing in the air, surely someone as utterly divine, as accomplished and confident as Ciro Delgato couldn't possibly want to get to know someone as plain, unsure and downright mixed up as Harriet Farrell.

CHAPTER SEVEN

'CIRO!'

Harriet's smile was wide as she pulled open her front door to see him standing there, holding a large brown paper bag. Berating the fact that she didn't have her robe ready to pull on in case there was a knock at the door and a certain doctor decided to check how she was doing, she'd had to settle for pulling on a pair of shorts and praying that the two triangles of her bikini top kept at least the essential bits covered.

For the last few days Ciro had been playing the part of the dutiful neighbour and doctor to perfection, dropping in each evening to check on her progress, telling her off when, bright red, she'd answered the door having clearly fallen asleep in the sun. As boring as it must have been for Ciro, his visits were fast becoming the highlight of Harriet's day! Late spring-time at Coogee Beach was arguably the best place in the world for some serious recuperation of the soul, but there was only so much introspection Harriet could stomach, and any diversion, especially one as stunning as Ciro, was rather gratefully received.

'I wasn't sure if you were home.' Ciro gestured to the dark flat. 'I thought you might need these.'

The open door was clearly enough of an invitation for Ciro and he walked in. Harriet flicked on the light, watching open-mouthed as he proceeded to empty the bag.

'Red wine, chocolate, a very slushy DVD.' He held it up for her inspection and then carried on depositing his wares over the bench. 'More chocolate and a box of tissues.' He gave a triumphant smile. 'Now that you are physically on the mend, I figure it's time to start on the emotional so I've bought all the ingredients necessary for a woman who has a heart that is broken.'

'A broken heart, even!' Harriet grinned. 'What makes you such an expert on women?'

'I have three sisters,' Ciro groaned. 'So you can lose the sarcasm. Back home in Spain I do not have much of a first-aid kit in my hacienda, but I have a bag like this packed and ready in my pantry for when one of my sisters drops by unexpectedly or calls for me to come over urgently.'

'I'm sure you make a lovely agony aunt,' Harriet said, picturing the scene and heading over to the bench to eye the goodies. 'Yes, please, to the wine and chocolate and the DVD. Actually, this is one I've been meaning to get, but I won't be needing the tissues.'

'Harriet, you don't need to be brave.'

'I'm not being brave,' Harriet insisted. 'I'm doing fine.'

'Sitting in the dark, feeling sorry for yourself, is not doing fine,' Ciro pointed out.

'I was actually sitting on the balcony, watching a glorious sunset,' Harriet corrected him. 'And, before you suggest it, my lack of emotion has nothing to do with the fact I don't have your sisters' passionate Latin blood running through my veins. The simple matter is, I did all my crying over the end of my relationship long ago.'

'A week isn't very long,' Ciro pointed out.

'A year is, though.' She gave a small shrug, then wished she hadn't. Her tiny bikini was not really geared for shoulder movement and for a moment, so small it was barely there, she felt Ciro's gaze flick downwards, and about the same time her heart rate soared skywards. She was suddenly acutely aware of her lack of attire, and that she hadn't had a pert bust since pre-adolescence. Her very exposed breasts were jiggling around to a tune of their own and it would make it even more embarrassing if she suddenly dashed off, dropped the chocolate she had picked up and ran to the bedroom to throw on a T-shirt. Instead, she had to ride out the suddenly uncomfortable conversation, horribly conscious of the fact that, though newly tanned, her stomach could hardly be described as toned. 'I did all the emotional groundwork months ago. In fact, if I hadn't found Drew in bed with that woman, I don't doubt for a moment that I'd be exactly where I am now.' She registered his frown. 'I'd decided we were both going to face up to it once I was feeling better, even as I was riding home in the taxi…' Her voice trailed off. Over it she may be, but that didn't mean she wanted to relive it just yet.

'Would you like some wine?' Ciro offered after a suitably long pause, realising she wasn't about to elaborate. Probably because his apartment was the same as hers, when she nodded her acceptance, he was able to locate the corkscrew and glasses with ease. 'Why don't we try and catch the end of that sunset?'

Grabbing a flimsy wrap from the sofa, Harriet led him onto her balcony, grateful for the spectacular pink sky that surpassed any need for small talk. Watching in amicable silence as the sun dipped lower, listening to the raucous laughter of some teenagers partying on the beach, sipping on her wine, feeling the warmth of the liquid spreading through her, the exquisite shyness of having him so near finally abated enough to allow her to steal a glimpse of his haughty profile.

'It is very beautiful,' Ciro said, staring out into the distance. And Harriet murmured her agreement, only she wasn't talking about the sunset. 'Sydney really is very beautiful.'

'It is,' Harriet agreed, because with the stars so low you could almost touch them, with the sound of laughter and scents of garlic and herbs winging their way up from the bars and cafés along the foreshore, it would, quite simply, be impossible not to. 'I didn't think so at first, though,' Harriet admitted. 'I wasn't looking forward to moving here at all.'

'How long have you been here?'

'Six months.' She took a sip of her wine before continuing. 'Six months has been about par for the course for the last few years. Every time I started to feel at home, every time I made a few friends, another role would come up, the next big thing Drew simply had to chase.' Realising she was running the risk of sounding as if she felt sorry for herself, Harriet adopted a more positive note to her voice. 'It worked, though. I mean, he started off in Perth with mainly walk-on non-talking parts and the occasional advert, then he took a part in Queensland on one of the local children's shows as co-presenter, which got him noticed.'

'Where to then?'

'Melbourne. He got a fairly big part in a soap, and from there he was invited to play the roles he's doing now, but it meant another move.'

'And how did you feel about all these moves?' Ciro asked.

Harriet gave a tight shrug. 'Nursing's very portable.'

'I know that,' Ciro said patiently, 'but how did *you* feel about constantly moving?'

'Exhausted,' Harriet admitted. 'Perhaps the most stupid part of the whole fiasco is that finally we seemed settled, geographically of course. Drew's career was really taking off. For the first time in our marriage suddenly we weren't dependent on my wage. I was even thinking about…' She didn't finish, shaking her head in the darkness, determined not to get maudlin, determined not to dwell on the could-have-beens that simply weren't.

But Ciro wasn't about to be fobbed off.

'What were you thinking about doing?'

'It doesn't matter now,' Harriet started, but she realised there was nothing maudlin about what she was thinking—in fact, it didn't even involve Drew. And there was something infinitely patient about Ciro, something so refreshingly open and direct about him that somehow, and not for the first time, she found herself opening up.

'You know how I told you I spent some time on an adolescent psychiatric unit? Well, it really had a huge impact on me.'

'Were you thinking of doing psychiatric nursing?'

Harriet shook her head, blushing at her own presumption as she voiced her dreams, wondering what a very senior doctor's take would be on them. 'I wanted to study psychology, maybe one day specialise in people like Alyssa.'

And he didn't give a patronising smile, or stare at her as if she were having some sort of manic delusion. He just gave a thoughtful nod. 'You did very well with her—with her mother, too.'

'That's the part that interests me,' Harriet responded eagerly. 'The whole family dynamics, the bigger picture, not just what happened to, say, Alyssa, but what happened to her mother. Why her mother is so compelled…' Her voice trailed off. She was embarrassed by her own enthusiasm but Ciro didn't seem to mind a bit.

'Alyssa spoke with me about you. She said you were very kind to her when she was on EHU.'

'You've been to see her?'

'A couple of times.' Ciro nodded. 'Though I'll probably leave it for a couple of weeks. I don't want her getting too dependent. You have to be very careful…' It was Ciro's voice trailing off now, Ciro giving a tight shrug, clearly trying to end the conversation.

'You seem to know a lot about it,' Harriet observed, her eyes narrowing slightly as she watched his reaction. 'More than most emergency doctors, perhaps?'

Almost reluctantly he nodded.

'My twin sister, Nikki—'

'You're a twin!'

'Yes, and we are very close. But Nikki suffers from an eating disorder. I have been through many hospital admissions with Nikki, so I know how hard the first few days can be. That is why I warned Alyssa that it might be exceptionally difficult for her on EHU. Staff on a general ward, no matter how good their intentions, just don't understand that the entire body image and emotional thought processes of people with eating disorders are chronically distorted—that it's about so much more than food.'

'It must be hard for you,' Harriet observed, 'seeing someone you love so much suffering.' But Ciro shook his head.

'If it's been hard for me then it's been unbearable for

Nikki. She is doing so well now, has fought her way back, but it isn't something that can be cured as such. Every day is a fresh challenge. She has to be constantly vigilant, to recognise when old habits start creeping in…' He gave a small smile, but it was loaded with pain. 'But you already know this, don't you?'

'I know a bit,' Harriet admitted. 'I'd like to know more.'

'You'd be very good.'

'Would have been very good,' Harriet corrected. 'I was accepted to study psychology at uni a few years ago, but at the time we couldn't afford it.' This time Ciro did raise his eyebrows. 'OK, Drew wasn't getting much work and we really needed a full-time wage. But when we moved here and his work was more secure…' She shook her head. 'It doesn't matter.'

'So what has changed?' Ciro asked. 'You can't deny this is a new chapter in your life. Why not go the whole way and do something that you really want to?'

'I might,' Harriet said tightly. 'Just not yet.'

But from his frown, Harriet realised he didn't understand, just didn't get the emotional war zone her life had been for so long now, still would be for a while yet, at least until her divorce came through. He couldn't comprehend the battering her confidence had taken over and over, that apart from nursing every facet of her life had changed.

'I want some peace,' Harriet said finally. 'I'm tired of unpacking boxes only to pack them up again a few months later, tired of being interviewed for a job I've been doing for years and starting over in yet another hospital, tired of having my mail redirected, or when the car needs a service having to find yet another new garage…' Now she *was* starting to sound sorry for herself so she lightened it with a very bright smile. 'I like Sydney,' Harriet said firmly. 'I love the fact that the beaches are just a stone's throw from the city, love the ferries leaving the harbour, and the cafés and the mass of people, love the fact that at five a.m. at the end of a night shift I can go up to the top floor and watch the sunrise on a new day.'

'It sounds like you're staying!'

'I am,' Harriet said firmly, but taken aback a touch by her sudden decision. 'I like my job, like the people I'm working with, and for the first time in years I'm going to stay put. Who knows? When the dust has settled, maybe I will go to uni and do psychology.'

'Just not yet?' Ciro ventured, and Harriet nodded.

'Just not yet. Thanks for this.' Holding up her wine-glass, she chinked it with his. 'It's nice to have a sympathetic ear.'

'Harriet, I am not here just to offer sympathy.' Those gorgeous mocha-coloured eyes were staring directly at her. 'I am here to spend some time with you, to get to know you. I am not very good at hiding my feelings and until I knew that you were sure your marriage was over it would not have been appropriate for me to come around for anything more than a very brief visit.'

'Appropriate?'

'I have watched you on the beach.' Ciro gestured to the vast expanse below. 'Seen the indecision in you…'

'Ciro, there was no indecision, just pain.'

'You needed space,' Ciro said firmly, and Harriet had to leave it at that, but knew that the second she was alone she would go over the words he had said and see, if on replay, they were as wonderful as they sounded now, if Ciro was really saying that he wanted to spend time with her, not as a colleague, not as a neighbour, but as a woman.

And it should surely have been the most nerve-racking evening of her life, but it wasn't, and it had nothing to do with two glasses of wine and everything to do with this amazing, insightful man. A man who actually knew not just how to listen but what to say, too, making her laugh, regaling stories of his own. And by the time the mozzies had started making themselves known and the noise from the party on the beach became more raucous than high-spirited it seemed the most natural thing in the world to drift into the lounge to relax back on the sofa and break open the chocolate while watching what would surely now top the list as Harriet's all-time favourite movie.

'You know it's really over when you sleep in the middle of the bed,' Ciro said authoritatively, handing her a tissue at a particularly tragic part, because when it was someone else's life that was in tatters it was easier to cry somehow, easier to let go of the tears and pass them off for someone else.

'I already am,' Harriet gulped, startled that he had voiced something she had already thought about. It had actually come as a pleasant surprise to find that the bed wasn't too big without Drew—in fact, it was divine, lying in the middle, stretching like a cat as she awakened with the sun. 'The very first day I moved in here—that night I moved to the middle.'

'There's no going back, then,' Ciro said assuredly. 'Only forward—at least, that is what my sisters tell me.'

'You have three sisters?' Finding her voice she resumed the earlier conversation.

'Three very different sisters,' Ciro elaborated. 'Cara is the eldest, impossibly dreamy and with the most appalling taste in men—married, drinkers, gamblers. I tell her one day she'll hit the jackpot and manage to in-corporate all three in the same guy. Estelle is studious, swore she'd never settle down until she'd finished her PHD, but she fell in love with a fellow student and now has two daughters, and we found out last week she is expecting twins—girls,' he added. 'All my life I am surrounded by women. Do you know that ginger cats are always male?'

'I think so,' Harriet said, raking her memory and trying to revive this rather useless piece of information.

'My mother bought one for me, supposedly to even things up—it had kittens a few months later!'

'Gosh!' Harriet blinked. No wonder he was so good with women, the poor guy was surrounded by them. 'What about Nikki? How is she?'

'She is doing great now, busy working and getting on with her life.'

'What work does she do?'

'She models, which is not the ideal environment for someone who is so delicate, but she seems to be coping well at the moment.'

So good looks clearly ran in the family.

'And these sisters of yours.' Harriet took a gulp of wine, nervously broaching a subject she desperately wanted answers to while hoping to sound somehow casual. 'When your relationships end, do they do the mercy dash with chocolate and wine and slushy movies?'

'Oh, no!' Ciro shook his head firmly.

'Too proud to cry?'

'No.' Ciro shook his head again. 'I am not one for regrets, for thinking what might have been.' He dusted his hands together in a gesture of finality. 'If it's over, it's over.'

'Ouch!'

He laughed as she flinched. 'It is much better that way. Most of my ex-girlfriends are still friends of mine. What?' he asked as Harriet shot him a disbelieving look. 'You don't believe me—but they really are!' Ciro insisted. 'Just because we are no longer in a relationship it doesn't mean we cannot still be friends.'

'Ciro.' She couldn't help but smile, a tiny sigh of sympathy escaping her lips for all his ex-girlfriends, because, as sure as eggs were eggs, one night in Ciro Delgato's arms would render any friendship null and void. 'I guarantee these so-called *friends* of yours don't see it that way. In fact, I'd bet that these friends of yours would tumble into bed with you at a moment's notice.'

'Of course!' He wasn't remotely embarrassed and Harriet's mouth dropped open at his shameless honesty. 'So long as neither of us are in a relationship, where is the harm?'

'I don't know,' Harriet said feebly, suddenly feeling horribly unsophisticated. 'It just seems so…pointless, I guess. I mean you know it isn't going to work out…'

'Harriet, do you read books again?'

'Sorry?'

'You have a favourite book that your read over and over?'

'Yes,' Harriet agreed faintly.

'Even though you know the ending, those books you once adored can still give you pleasure.'

'Book,' Harriet corrected briskly. 'I have one favourite book that occasionally I take down and read again, and then I wonder why I bothered because as it turns out, the ending is absolutely horrible! Personally I'd rather explore pastures new than visit old haunts…'

'I'm teasing you, Harriet.' He smiled a delicious,

lazy smile. 'And you are very easy to tease. But I am friends with some of my exes, though not Lana.' He gave a slight wince. 'That one did hurt a bit.'

'Sorry.'

'Don't be.' Ciro shrugged. 'Now I realise we're better apart. Lana didn't want a relationship, more someone on her arm looking good.' Somehow Ciro could say it without it sounding boastful, and most amazingly of all Harriet actually understood.

'Drew was the same. Not at first, of course, but as he got more successful more and more he wanted the trophy wife.'

Ciro gave a knowing nod. 'Someone to look the part!'

'Or, in my case, not looking the part,' Harriet sighed. 'I never quite managed to look like the gorgeous wife Drew so badly wanted.'

'But you are gorgeous,' Ciro said as if it were fact, as if it were absolutely unequivocal. She waved him away, stood up, collected the wineglasses and empty bottle and headed for the kitchenette, sure that gorgeous wasn't the word he was looking for, that his mental Spanish to English thesaurus had somehow misinterpreted the word. Nice? Perhaps. Friendly? Maybe. On a good day she could even muster passably attractive, but she was definitely *not* gorgeous.

'You are,' Ciro insisted, walking in behind her, and suddenly the simple became terribly complicated. Rinsing two glasses under the tap and putting the wine bottle in the recycle bin took a mammoth effort of concentration. 'And, no, I have not got my words mixed up,' he said, reading her mind. 'It was the first thing I thought when I saw you.'

'What was the second?' Harriet asked, embarrassed

but pleased, and scarcely able to comprehend that she was prolonging this dangerous conversation, scarcely able to believe she was pushing further.

'Married.' Picking up her hand, he held it, brushing her newly naked ring finger. 'And I'm sure you can guess the third thing I thought.'

'No.' Harriet swallowed, because she could *hope* she knew the third thing Ciro had thought, could hope that this stunning, sensual man had truly been disappointed by the sight of a ring on her finger. But until he said it, until she heard those words coming from his full, very close mouth, she didn't dare to believe it.

'Damn,' Ciro said slowly. 'And that's the polite version.'

'Really?'

'Really,' Ciro murmured, and she could have sworn he was about to kiss her, his eyes narrowing in thought as he stared down at her. 'Should I go?' She could hear the question in his voice as he smiled down at her, could feel the lust thrumming in the air as he continued to stare, his mouth a mere breath away. She knew he was offering her an out, only Harriet didn't want it.

His hand still warm and dry around hers, his face was moving closer but Harriet stood still. In that tiny slice of time her mind processed a multitude of thoughts, a flurry of internal conflict, as his other hand coiled around her waist, slipping under the flimsy fabric of her wrap and meeting the warm sun-kissed flesh, his fingers softly stroking her spinal column, running shivers the entire length of her body, every slow, measured move accelerating her heart rate.

Her eyes wide in a strange sensual terror.

This could only end in tears—hers.

It was too soon, way too soon.

Surely it could never, ever work.

But she needed this. With blinding clarity Harriet realised she needed this more than the air she was breathing—needed to experience the weight of his mouth on hers, to feel as divine and gorgeous as Ciro made her feel, to be kissed, tasted, wanted. And if it couldn't work, she'd just live for the moment. If she was heading for a fall, for now she'd enjoy the ride.

A hastily drawn-up contract with her inner soul was penned in a nanosecond!

His breath was dusting her cheeks, the heat from his palm radiating through the small of her back, his mere touch, his very presence in her personal space so exquisitely sensual Harriet could feel the heavy stir of her own arousal, and his lips hadn't even met hers. Could feel her breasts swell, filling the Lycra triangles, her nipples straining against the flimsy fabric, her stomach liquid churning to the pulsing beat between her legs. And now it wasn't just Ciro moving closer but Harriet, too, her eyes closing in dizzy anticipation, but nothing could have prepared her for the impact of his searching lips on hers.

It had been for ever since she'd been kissed.

Really kissed.

With Drew, more and more it had been a perfunctory thing, had made her feel as sensual as an old maiden aunt with a hairy chin that one was forced to kiss at Christmas—the only thing he hadn't done had been to wipe his mouth on the back of his hand afterwards. Yet with Ciro it was as if he couldn't get enough of her, tongues mingling, lips swelling against each other. And not just lips. The drag of his rough unshaven skin against her cheek, pulling the soft skin, the utter size of him engulfing her, holding her fiercely, making her feel more of a woman than she had ever felt.

And if this was a rebound, Harriet gasped as his hand pulled her closer, as she felt the muscular firmness of his thighs pressing against hers, the swollen heat of his arousal nudging into her stomach, if this was a rebound then bring it on. If this was the cure for a broken heart, balm for raw wounds, then she wanted it, needed it.

Faint with longing, she mumbled with protest as he pulled away, her lips stinging, her body alive.

'I have to go,' Ciro said in that low, husky drawl that had her insides turning.

'Do you?' It was bold and it was brave and it was completely out of character, but it was exactly how he made her feel, caution thrown to the wind. But Ciro deftly caught it and handed it softly back.

'I do,' he said slowly, as he stared down at her, his eyes infinitely kind, taking away the sting of embarrassment at her earlier boldness. 'And you have to be very sure that this is what you want.'

She did want.

But in a flash of self-preservation Harriet didn't voice it, just nodded back at him, chewing on her bottom lip as he went on.

'This has been a wonderful evening, Harriet, and it would be very easy to…' He gave a small shrug. Maybe he didn't know the right word, or maybe he knew that if he voiced it, made it real, then it would be even harder just to walk away. 'I don't just want to console you, Harriet. Do you understand what I'm saying?'

Dumbly she nodded, watching as he picked up his keys and left.

Heading back onto the balcony, Harriet sat in the darkness hugging her knees to her chest, listening to lapping waves. Slowly her breathing evened, slowly sensibility crept in, bravado fading with every passing second.

Ciro might be worried that she'd regret it in the morning, that this was a mere rebound, but Harriet already knew from just one kiss that it was way more than that.

Pulling her wrap tighter around her shoulders, she shivered for a moment, the absolute magnitude of what was taking place only just starting to hit home.

Ciro had been right to halt things, he had been right to insist that they take things slowly.

It would be so very easy to fall.

But almost impossible to get up again.

CHAPTER EIGHT

'HARRIET!'

The same voice that filled her dreams was summoning her from sleep, a loud banging on the door snapping her into consciousness. Harriet stumbled out of bed, desperately trying to orientate herself, recognising the urgency in Ciro's voice, that frantic call for assistance she had heard from more doctors than she could remember.

But she wasn't at work.

It took a moment to find the light switch, a moment to comprehend that this wasn't a dream and that she wasn't at work, that she wasn't even at home, but it was definitely Ciro knocking loudly at her door and from the urgency in his voice this was no time to try and locate her gown.

'Harriet!' His shout didn't fade as she flung open the door draped only in a bathroom towel, blinking at the bright hall lights of the apartment block, squinting at Ciro who was crouched in her doorway equally suitably undressed in a pair of dark boxers. He was pulling on a pair of runners. 'Those kids that were partying on the beach…' Footwear on, he was heading for the stairwell, giving her just enough information to act before he bolted down the stairs. 'I've called for an ambulance, they're in trouble.'

And that was all the information she needed. Berating the fact she wasn't tidier, Harriet located her shorts from her bedroom floor and pulled them on before yanking open her chest of drawers and grabbing the first T-shirt that came to hand. For the sake of speed and safety she followed Ciro's cue and spent thirty seconds pulling on her own runners so she could race down the stairs and out into the night. The air was cool now, the foreshore eerily dark without the familiar glow of the cafés. There were just a few streetlights to guide the way. The moon was hidden behind low clouds, bobbing out occasionally to give Harriet a view of what lay in store as she ran along the beach. And it wasn't a pretty sight.

Ciro, waist-deep in the water, was diving in, swimming towards a surfboard that an exhausted swimmer was trying to drag to shore, an inert body lying, floppy and prone, on it. Harriet knew, even from this distance, that the victim was in serious trouble. However, causing her even more concern right now was the group of hysterical teenagers that were shouting and swaying on the beach, screaming frantically for Ciro to hurry, one even trying to run into the inky water. Harriet was genuinely concerned that this already bad situation could turn into a complete disaster.

'Stop him,' Harriet shouted, pointing to the drunk teenager who was already knee-deep. But her voice was carried away in the wind. Her only option was to run faster, to stop him before he drowned himself.

Accelerating harder, her breath caught in her lungs, the salty air stung her nostrils, her heart pounded in her chest, and she tried to ignore the pull of her recent stitches as she stretched the boundaries of gentle post-operative exercise.

She could feel the waves whipping around her ankles and already her trainers were making running even heavier. But if she wanted to stop him there wasn't time to take them off. The ground suddenly shifted beneath her, the water waist-high now, and Harriet took a final lunge at the young man, deciding in her own mind that if she couldn't reach him there was no way she was going in any further, the water was just too deep, the surge too strong for her in her already exhausted state.

'Get back to shore.' His arm was wet under her grip, shrugging her off.

'I want to help.'

'Not this way,' she shouted. 'They're bringing him in. That man's a doctor. You're going to end up needing to be rescued yourself.'

Mercifully he didn't take another step out, but neither was he heading back to the safety of the shore, and Harriet knew she only had a small window of time to persuade him before foolish bravado took over and he headed back out.

'You can help him,' Harriet shouted, 'by going to the street and directing the ambulance.'

'But Vince needs his mates.'

'He needs medical help,' Harriet said urgently. She was freezing now, struggling to keep her footing. 'You need to wave them down and show them exactly where we are. Come on,' she insisted, heading back to the shore and praying he would follow her lead.

After a small hesitation he saw sense, wading through the waves to his waiting friends, urging them to the street. But Harriet's real work had barely started. Ciro was swimming back now with the other rescuer, both men attempting to guide the surfboard, but Harriet could see it was growing increasingly difficult as they neared the shore, the breaking waves making the task more difficult. She watched with her heart in her mouth, knowing from her brief foray in the water just how exhausted Ciro and the rescuer must be, but knowing that unless they hurried they weren't going to make it back in time, that already it might be too late to save this victim.

'Stay there, love.'

Sheer relief flooded her as she heard the welcome sound of reinforcements. Three burly men, alerted by the distressed teenagers, were rushing past her, heading out just as Ciro had done, with no thought for their own safety, willing to help a stranger in trouble. And many hands did make light work. They dragged the victim those last exhausting metres and as they lifted him out of the water, not for the first time Harriet thanked her lucky stars that these men had arrived. The victim was a thick-set, burly guy and it would have been an almost impossible feat in Ciro's and the rescuer's depleted state to drag him the last few metres to where Harriet was waiting. Wasting no time, Harriet set to work, sweeping his airway clear, palpating his neck for a pulse and then pinching his nostrils and extending his neck. She delivered two swift breaths into the patient before commencing cardiac massage.

'I'm coming.' Ciro was nearby, his hands on his knees, coughing, choking on the salty water that must surely be filling his lungs, trying to somehow summon the energy to complete the task.

'I'm OK,' Harriet said, pushing on the large chest, but though her words were brave she needed help. This guy was big. It took a huge physical effort to effectively massage his chest and all her breath was taken up giving him the kiss of life. She could feel the pull of her incision, knew she couldn't keep this up for much longer.

'Where the hell's the ambulance?' Harriet called, between expirations.

'It's coming,' someone shouted. 'I can hear the sirens.'

But Harriet couldn't hear anything except the sound of her own pulse pounding in her temples, the scorching sting of every breath as she worked on. Even though he was nowhere near ready, Ciro must have recognised her desperation because he knelt down beside her and pushed her hand away, not wasting a single precious breath to tell her he was taking over, just extending his arms and pushing down hard on the man's chest. Harriet moved up to the head, her eyes trained on Ciro's hands, watching for the tiny pause so she could push in her exhaled air.

'Stop.' Feeling a shudder of resistance, Harriet pulled her face back, placed her hand on Ciro's arm and they both leant back on their heels. Ciro's fingers palpated Vince's neck, concentration etched on every feature as he strained to find a pulse, but it seemed useless. Just as Harriet was sure she must somehow have imagined the tiny shift in tone she'd felt in the young man, suddenly his chest moved and he spluttered, his whole body convulsing in spasms as Harriet and Ciro swiftly rolled him onto his side, Ciro pushing on his back to force out the salty water that was choking him.

'OK, guys, help's here.'

Harriet didn't know the paramedics who had arrived, but relief flooded her at the sight of the bright green uniforms, the shiny boxes they dropped silently onto the sand. She noted with a wry smile that Ciro didn't waste time stating the obvious. He just gave a very brief handover and introduction as the paramedics set to work assessing the patient and attaching him to monitors and blood pressure equipment. Harriet silently assisted.

'He was in full arrest by the time we got him to shore.' Ciro gestured over to the other rescuer, still lying on the beach, his mates now surrounding him. 'He needs to be seen at the hospital—that guy must have swallowed half the ocean.'

'How long were you giving CPR before he responded?'

'Unfortunately I'm not wearing my watch, but five, maybe seven minutes.' Ciro looked at Harriet for confirmation and she nodded. Happy to hand over, but still willing to participate, she unravelled the oxygen tubing and slipped the mask over the man's face as Ciro took the paramedics' stethoscope while one inserted an IV bung, shaking his head as he listened to the patient's chest.

'Poor air entry, he's making only minimal respiratory effort.'

And there was a decision to be made—to scoop and run and take him to the hospital, which was a few minutes' drive away at breakneck speed where skilled help and equipment was waiting, or to intubate the patient here, knowing that at any time Vince could arrest again or suffer another seizure.

'His oxygen saturation is only eighty-five per cent,' one of the paramedics called. 'What do you want to do, Doc?'

'Intubate,' Ciro said after only the briefest of hesitations. Clearly the paramedics agreed with his decision and wasted no time in handing Ciro the necessary equipment as Harriet applied crico-thyroid pressure—pressing on the patient's neck to allow for easier insertion of the tube.

'His air entry is better now,' Ciro said, listening to the chest again. 'I think we should get him to Emergency now. Do you want me to let them know?'

'We can do that. Are you coming for the ride, Doc?' the paramedic asked. But another ambulance was pulling up now, more assistance arriving with each passing minute. The emergency was under control now and Ciro finally relaxed, a rueful smile appearing on his exhausted face.

'Preferably no!' He gestured to his drenched boxer shorts and now bare feet. 'I'm sure you guys can take it from here.' Standing up, he took a moment to shake the paramedics' hands firmly. 'You've done a great job. Thank you for your prompt assistance.'

'No worries,' one of the paramedics answered, lifting the stretcher, the wheels not exactly designed for the soft sand. 'It's going to be nice working with you, Doctor.'

The other team was tending to the rescuer, wrapping him in blankets, reassuring Vince's friend as the police arrived and started to make their enquiries, taking statements from the witnesses.

'Here you go!' A thick blanket was being placed around Harriet's shoulders. Still kneeling on the sand, she was too tired even to offer her thanks and shivered violently, vaguely aware of Ciro talking to police officers as a paramedic knelt down beside her. 'Are you OK?'

Harriet nodded, her teeth chattering too violently to attempt an answer, shock and fatigue starting to set in.

'You've cut yourself,' the paramedic observed, shining his torch down her legs. Harriet vaguely recalled the sharp pain that had shot through her as she'd knelt down. She stared down at her leg as if it belonged to someone else as he carefully examined it. 'Looks like it was glass, there's a few broken bottles lying around. Let's get you into the ambulance and get you to the hospital…'

'I don't need to go to hospital,' Harriet managed, but something in her voice must have alerted Ciro. He swung around, forgetting the conversation he was having with the police officer and coming straight over.

'What's wrong?'

'Nothing.' Harriet coughed, wishing they would all leave her alone. 'I'm cold, that's all.'

'She's got a laceration on her leg…'

'I've got a small cut on my leg,' Harriet corrected him, but Ciro was dropping down on his own knees now, running a concerned, trained eye over her.

'She had an appendicectomy last week,' Ciro said to the hovering paramedic.

'*She* can speak for herself,' Harriet retorted.

'She's also a terribly uncooperative patient.' Again he spoke over her, but there was a hint of humour that softened it, his eyes narrowing in concern as he eyed her more closely. 'What is wrong, Harriet?'

And he said it so softly, so gently she felt a sting of tears in her eyes. The night's events, the week's events, the entire wretched last few months finally catching up with her. 'I'm cold and I'm tired and I just want to go…' The tears came then, tears she had held back for so long now, tears she had sworn no one would ever see. But sitting on a beach, wrapped in an ambulance blanket, at two a.m. only compounded her sudden chaotic existence, only served to enforce her desolation.

Ciro thankfully understood, realised that her tears and overwhelming lethargy were more emotional than physical, that the very last thing she needed right now was to be hauled back to hospital, to fan the flames she was so desperately trying to put out.

'Let's get you *home*.' He said the last word very deliberately. His strong hand gently guided her up and he pulled her into his chest, he held her closely as he addressed the police officer.

'I have told you all I can. If you need anything more from me you can contact me at the hospital.'

'If you can just tell us when you first became aware—?' the young officer started, but Ciro wasn't listening.

One strong arm around Harriet, he guided her slowly along the beach towards the apartments and called over his shoulder, 'This can all wait until tomorrow.'

They took the lift in silence, Ciro's arm still wrapped around her, still holding her tightly against him. Somewhere between the second and third floors he wasn't just someone to lean on, somewhere around the fourth the heart pounding in her ears was Ciro's, not hers. As he held her to his chest, she could feel the quiet masculine strength of him, the smooth velvet of his chest against her cheek, the slight scratch of hair as he pulled her even closer, and she knew without looking that they were bypassing her floor, that they were going back to Ciro's apartment.

'I'm going to run you a warm bath and then take a look at you.' Leading her over to the sofa, he unwrapped her from the blanket.

Harriet gingerly sat down, casting a shy eye around the room.

His apartment was the image of hers, exactly the same floor plan, the furniture almost identical, yet it was an entirely different dwelling. Somehow he had masculinised it, the tangy citrus of aftershave hanging in the air, a mountain of newspapers on the coffee-table, his tie and jacket tossed messily over the chair and endless coffee-cups filling the sink.

'Your bath is ready.' He was back, smiling that

familiar professional smile, and Harriet almost physically ached for earlier, not the earlier downstairs in her own apartment but back in the lift, when he had held her in his arms, when he had dragged her into his personal space, his touch the only comfort that would suffice. But it would be dangerous to let him see that, dangerous to head down that path in a weak and vulnerable moment. It was far easier to paint on a smile, far easier to reassure him that she was fine.

'I really am OK.' She was feeling more like her old self now. The exquisite loneliness that had assailed her on the beach had abated and Harriet felt almost foolish for lowering her guard, guilty even that she had worried him. 'I was just in such a deep sleep when you knocked, I didn't have time to process it…'

'You've had a shock,' Ciro explained, the voice of reason, but Harriet shook her head.

'I work in Emergency, Ciro. It's hardly the first time I've given CPR.'

'There's a big difference between a well-stocked emergency room with doctors and nurses on tap and a beach in the middle of the night.'

Almost reluctantly she nodded.

'You've just recovered from surgery,' Ciro continued. 'You're supposed to be resting.'

'Hey, you were the one who knocked!'

'And I'd do it again tomorrow,' Ciro answered, 'but that doesn't mean—' The ringing of the telephone halted his little lecture, but from the expletive that escaped his lips Harriet guessed he wasn't particularly impressed at the intrusion.

'Aren't you going to get it?' Harriet asked, frowning as Ciro shook his head. 'It might be the hospital.'

'The hospital rings me on my mobile…' Finally he

answered the call and Harriet feigned disinterest, looked anywhere but at Ciro as he spoke curtly into the telephone, letting the poor unfortunate on the other end know exactly what he thought of their early morning greeting.

'My sister!' Replacing the phone in its cradle, Ciro turned his palms skywards. 'She still hasn't worked out the time difference between Spain and Australia. Now, where were we?'

'I was about to have a bath,' Harriet answered, more brightly than she felt. Something about the telephone call had unsettled her, yet she couldn't quite place what. But there wasn't time to dwell on it as Ciro halted her progress as she attempted to stand.

'Not so fast. I need to have a look at you first. Is your stomach still hurting?'

'A bit,' Harriet admitted. 'But I don't think it's anything serious. I could feel my incision pulling when I was running and while I was doing the massage. I'm sure I just did too much.'

'What about your knee?' he asked, gently probing the bruised, cut flesh as Harriet frowned down at him.

'Why do you talk to your sister in English?' She watched as his fingers stilled momentarily, an almost imperceptible pause before he carried on examining her, his answer when it came vague and dismissive.

'I forget where I am sometimes.'

His touch on her skin was almost more than she could bear and it had nothing to do with her injuries and everything to do with his utter tenderness. In an attempt at self-preservation, she jerked her knee away.

'It's a tiny cut, Ciro, nothing to make a fuss about!'

'OK.' He gave a wan smile. 'You really are a terrible patient, you know.'

'Because I hate being one,' Harriet mumbled. 'Can I just have my bath, please?'

'When I've seen your stomach.' Ciro was insistent. 'If you've torn anything, the last thing you need is to step into a hot bath.'

It made sense, enough sense for Harriet to lie back on the sofa, enough sense to let him lift her legs up. She wriggled her body straight, tried to keep her breathing even as for the second time Ciro's hands probed her stomach. Only this time she wasn't concentrating on holding her stomach in, she'd have settled for keeping her breathing even. His hands probed her tender flesh as she stared fixedly at the ceiling.

'Your shorts.' Ciro's voice was even, his fingers fiddling with the tiny silver catch, but Harriet pushed them away, dealing with the fastening herself and wiggling her hips as best she could, moving the damp, unyielding garment down an inch so he could see her wound.

'Harriet, I need to examine your stomach properly.'

She had known it wasn't enough, had known that he needed her shorts to be properly loosened to adequately examine her scar, and she held her breath as his fingers moved the zipper down an inch, that tiny distance enough to allow for a proper examination of her abdomen. If Ciro had thought about it, he'd probably have realised that she wouldn't be wearing knickers. If he'd actually stopped to think, Ciro would have realised that when he'd knocked on her door an hour or so earlier and told her a kid was drowning, rummaging through her drawers for a pair of undies would have been the last thing on her mind. But clearly, from his reaction, from the loaded, charged atmosphere, he hadn't thought. Harriet felt it as if it was physical—the tiny beat of hesitation as the zipper opened, as his eyes took in that first glimpse of her golden curls, and the mood that was highly charged suddenly shifted to electric. If he'd been a doctor before, he wasn't now.

Her eyes dragged the length of his naked torso, taking in the same body she'd worked alongside for the last hour, but it was as if she was seeing it for the first time. The smattering of dark hair fanning his chest, so exquisitely masculine, snaking down his flat, toned stomach, down, ever down to the dark silky boxers, the hemline straining against his muscular thighs, tiny coils of hairs on his legs that she ached to reach out and feel, dizzy now, not with exhaustion or expended emotion but with sheer unadulterated lust.

And Ciro felt the shift, too, she knew that, knew that from the slight tremor in his hand, the tension in his throat as he swallowed.

'Does it hurt?'

'No.'

'Here?' His voice was thick with lust but at least he could speak.

The answer strangled in her throat. Instead, she shook her head against the cushion, not staring up at the ceiling as she had the last time he'd examined her but staring brazenly into his eyes, not willing this moment over but shamefully wishing it would never end. She could see the lust blazing in his eyes, feel the heat of his palm on her stomach, the coolness as he took it away.

'Harriet?'

She heard the question in his voice, knew that even at this late stage he was somehow trying to protect her from herself. He took her hand and led her to the bathroom and she knew that he wouldn't be leaving her alone. It had always been excruciating, undressing in front of a man, but Ciro dealt with that, undressing her himself with such utter reverence, his eyes adoring her as he slipped her shorts over her bottom, sliding them down her legs. She lifted her arms as docile as a sleepy child as he tugged off her T-shirt, the approval in his eyes as the temporary darkness lifted making her feel truly beautiful.

'It will feel hot.' Guiding her into the bath, he spoke softly to her. 'But that is just because you are cold. The water is just warm…'

'You're cold, too,' Harriet whispered, wincing when the biting water flamed her frozen flesh as she lowered her body into the stinging yet inviting heat. 'Why don't you—?'

'Let me look after you, Harriet.'

Dipping a sponge into the water, he squeezed it around her neck, rivers of warmth running down her spine. He moved the sponge along her frozen arms in slow, ever-decreasing circles of warmth, even massaging her hands, taking each finger in turn, instilling warmth where there had been none.

'Your knee.' He squeezed the sponge again and she gave a tiny wince at the sting of the soapy water, but the pain was short-lived. Ciro guided the sponge lengthways now, his hand disappearing beneath the surface of the water and massaging her aching calves. And there was no rush, none at all, each feather-light stroke relaxing her more, yet moving her further into giddy submission. Sponge forgotten, he soaped his hands, his eyes adoring her. Strong fingers massaged the knots of tension from her shoulders, but as his hands moved lower everything changed. To that point it had been tender, blissfully sensual perhaps but loosely within the bounds of decency, but as he took the weight of her heavy, soapy breasts, she felt her throat constrict with desire, closed her eyes to the ecstasy of skilful fingers as they finally crossed that delicious line, his lips moving downwards in deep, throaty kisses along her neck, stealthily moving downwards with such slow, teasing precision Harriet could feed a needy moan welling in her throat, wanting, needing, desperate to feel his mouth around her nipples.

He obliged, taking the ripe, swollen delicacy in his mouth, his teeth gently nibbling her areola, the fizz of arousal coursing through her breasts. She wanted so badly to focus on the bliss but his hand was working up her legs. Tiny gasps of approval escaped her lips but her body was saying otherwise. Her thighs closed around the hand that was slowly inching upwards, stalling his decadent progress. Her hand captured his strong forearm in a vague attempt to push him away, scared almost to give in, unable to comprehend that this could be enough for him, that surely she must reciprocate, but a low throaty murmur dictated his pleasure, his mouth still working her breast but his hand hovering, stroking, softly stroking her thigh, patiently awaiting her total consent. Harriet gave in to him then, gave herself in a way she never had before, stopped trying to fight for control and willingly let him have it.

Completely.

Her legs wilfully parted, giving in to the delicious sensations he so skilfully inflicted, her neck arching, this slow delicious torture almost more than she could bear. Yet she didn't want it to ever end, could feel his finger probing, parting the tender, engorged flesh of her hood, locating her precious jewel, applying little beats of pressure that made her want to weep, while his tongue still circled her nipple, drawing it to its delicious, tender length then pausing, holding her quivering mound in his loving hand, adoring her with his eyes.

'I want to take you to bed…' His low drawl was as erotic as his touch. 'Since the moment I saw you, Harriet, it is all I have wanted to do.'

She understood, because she'd felt it, too, more than she'd even wanted to admit at the time, more than she'd dared acknowledge, but that stinging, brutal awareness she had felt had been undeniable. That it was culminating in this was inevitable almost.

He effortlessly scooped her up and carried her the short distance to the bedroom and she buried her face in his chest, tasting the salt of the ocean, revelling in the delicious scent of arousal. And Harriet knew she should have felt shy, should have felt naked and exposed as he laid her on the bed, but he imbued wanton confidence in her, the desire blazing in his eyes telling her she was doing OK. The pleasure was as much his as hers. Her needy hands tugged at his boxers, and she saw Ciro in full arousal. The sheer glorious naked strength of him gave her a shudder of nervous apprehension, and he sensed it.

'I won't hurt you, Harriet.' Kneeling on the bed, he cupped the peach of her buttocks in his hand and, leaning over, kissed his way down the length of her writhing body. Achingly slowly he explored her with his tongue and at the scratch of his face on her stomach, the feel of his thighs parting hers, Harriet's hands coiled in his jet hair. Her head thrashed on the pillow as he took her so close to the edge it was almost indecent, the fuse he had lit in the bathroom so damn close to detonation now that the knot of anxiety about accommodating him was replaced with sheer naked need, a need to have him inside her, to have him fill her. His name was a sob on her parted lips as she begged him to enter her, but even his skilful foreplay, her greedy anticipation of the moment didn't come close to the power of him inside her, that first delicious stab the trigger, her whole body toppling, a physical chain reaction so severe there was nothing she could do except go with it—moving with him, her calves around his waist, the sheen of his skin against her, her fingers pushing into his taut buttocks, greedy, desperate lips tasting his flesh as he bucked inside her. A frenzied convulsion engulfed her, a hot searing flush rushing along her spinal column, his buttocks tightening in the same rigid tune she moved to as he swelled further within her, spilled inside her. She'd never cried before while making love, but it was the only thing she could do now. The amassing of emotion, the sheer and utter release, followed by the tranquil post-coital bliss, culminating in quiet, cleansing tears. And through it all Ciro held her.

Held Harriet as if he'd never let her go.

CHAPTER NINE

COOGEE BEACH was arguably the best place in the
world to get over a broken relationship or even to
forge a new one!

Restaurants designed for lovers were on every corner,
subdued lighting and informal couches where you could
feed each other on today's early morning catches. Or
you could just wander along the busy streets and stop
at any one of the trendy cafés and watch the world go
by. But as Harriet's strength, along with her confidence,
returned more and more, they strayed from their haven,
taking endless beachside walks right up to Bondi, following the tracks, stopping along the way to marvel at
the sandstone, the colours so rich, from saffron-yellow
to burnt orange, that they looked as if they'd been
painted for effect, poking sticks into tiny rock pools or
just stopping a while, Ciro lying on his side, watching
with a lazy smile as Harriet popped seaweed.

'Your skin is like the sandstone!' Harriet gave him
a queer look and Ciro laughed. 'I meant the many
colours, not the texture. First it was pale, then pink,
then angry red…'

'Don't remind me.' Harriet winced, her lobster impression not quite a distant enough memory to joke about yet.

'But now it is…' His hand brushed the sand from her thigh, staring thoughtfully at the million freckles dusting her legs.

'Freckly,' Harriet said for him, just a touch uncomfortable under his scrutiny, wishing she could be as olive-skinned and as long-limbed as the Mediterranean beauties he was undoubtedly used to, still scarcely able to fathom that a man as stunning as Ciro, a man so used to delectable women, could really find her as beautiful as he regularly insisted that she was.

'Are you nervous about going back to work tomorrow?' His hand was still there, stroking the tiny blonde hairs upwards, causing tiny shivers of electricity at his mere touch. Harriet finally nodded.

'I feel like I've been away for months, not just two weeks.'

'A lot has happened in that time,' Ciro said, and Harriet forgot the seaweed she was idly popping and stared out at the crystal-clear water, one part of her wishing it was this time tomorrow, that her first awkward day back was over and done with, while the other wished that they could just stay like this for ever.

'What's everyone going to think? I know you tried to hide it from me…'

'Hide what?' Ciro asked, but from the way his foot was scuffing the sand Harriet knew he'd guessed what she was about to say! 'I read that newspaper, Ciro. The one you said hadn't arrived. Well, Judith rang to discuss it with me and I found it in the recycle bin—read for myself how I was so devastated that I took an overdose after I found them in bed together.'

'Judith rang you?' Ciro's annoyance was obvious.

'I'm glad she did. Someone at the hospital must have leaked it and we were trying to work out who.'

'Why do you think someone from the hospital spoke to the press? Surely it would be from Drew's PR.'

'I doubt it,' Harriet scoffed. 'Drew's hell-bent on keeping his image clean.'

'It was only two lines in the paper.' Ciro shrugged. 'And they only insinuated that you might have done that. Anyway, no one will have seen it.'

'Oh, please!' Harriet rolled her eyes. 'As much as it galls me to admit it, Drew is finally famous! OK, he's not an international celebrity, but here in Sydney he's pretty hot property, which means that me ending up in hospital the night we broke up…'

'The hospital you work in,' Ciro pointed out. 'And everyone there knows that you had appendicitis that night—you had an operation, for heaven's sake. No one thinks for a moment that you took an overdose. You've got nothing to worry about.'

'I guess,' Harriet sighed. 'That's exactly what Judith said. Anyway, she didn't just ring for that…' A tiny proud smile wobbled on the edge of her lips. 'There's an ANUM position coming up.'

'A what?' Ciro frowned.

'Associate Nurse Unit Manager,' Harriet explained. 'It's probably where I should be by now, but I've never really been in one place long enough to apply for a promotion before.'

'And are you going to?'

Swivelling her eyes to him, she gave an incredulous smile. 'Of course I'm going to!' Harriet announced. 'Why wouldn't I? I may not get it, but I'm thrilled Judith's even considering me.'

'Well, good luck!' It didn't sound particularly heartfelt, but he gave her a wide smile. 'You're going to be fine tomorrow.'

The frantic chewing on her bottom lip told Ciro she wasn't entirely convinced.

'What else is worrying you?'

'Nothing,' she answered quickly. Too quickly perhaps because Ciro's hand was still now, the idle stroking halting.

'Harriet?'

She heard the question mark, the summons for the truth, and taking a deep breath she finally faced him.

'Can we keep it quiet? About us, I mean?'

'If that is what you want.' Ciro nodded. 'We can keep it to ourselves for now.'

'It's just, I mean I know we only met that night, that we couldn't possibly have been seeing each other before—'

'That's fine, Harriet,' Ciro broke in, but Harriet was on a roll now, hoping that by somehow putting her jumbled thoughts into words they might even start to make sense.

'Drew and I had been washed up for ages, but people didn't know that. They're going to think it's just a fling or wonder how on earth…' Her voice trailed off and after the longest silence it was Ciro who finally spoke.

'Are you beginning to wonder?' he asked perceptively.

'No,' she said, but her voice was saying otherwise. 'No,' Harriet said again more firmly, hoping that if she could convince him she could convince herself. 'Of course not.'

'Harriet, we need to talk.' Ciro's voice was serious, using that low, slightly urgent tone he had occasionally used these last few days when he had tried to bring up the difficult subject of their future.

If there could even be a future.

And she knew without him voicing it the sheer impossibility of the situation they were in—that Ciro was from the other side of the world, they spoke different languages, that if, *if* this relationship proceeded then horrible choices would have to be made. She felt cold fingers of fear creeping around her heart, just as they always did when the conversation turned this way. She felt a horrible sense of foreboding that she truly wanted to ignore, but Ciro wasn't letting up, his deep, lyrical voice stabbing at her fragile mind. 'There are things we have to discuss. Both of us are in other places…' His fingers snapped in frustration as he struggled to find the right words, but Harriet didn't want to hear them.

'*Different* places,' Harriet snapped back, jumping up quickly, determined to end this conversation before it even started. 'Both of us are in different places right now. I know that, Ciro!'

'Harriet, please, I just want to talk.'

His was entirely the voice of reason, but Harriet shook her head.

'Can't it wait, Ciro? I'm starting to burn, sitting here…' She raked a hand through her hair, brushed some sand from her legs, pulled down at her T-shirt—anything other than looking at him, anything other than seeing again the exasperation in his eyes at her utter refusal to listen. 'I just want to get the next few days over with. I've got work to deal with, solicitor's appointments and real estate agents to deal with. Surely we can do this some other time? Surely?' she said again, finally forcing herself to look at him.

Relief whooshed over her when finally he reluctantly nodded. He took her hand and they wandered in silence back to the apartments, watching a crazed cocker spaniel chasing the surf, the sun prickling shoulders

Ciro would surely massage later. And she wished she could capture that moment, hold that slice of time in her hands and never move forward, keep it all as simple as it was when it was only the two of them.

'Are you hungry?'

Ciro was flicking through his mail-box, pulling out letters and idly wading through his mail, as Harriet pressed the button for the lift.

'Starving,' Ciro moaned. 'But I am thinking we should just call for room…' He paused, standing stock-still for a moment, his eyes fixed on an envelope before he finished his sentence. But to Harriet every word was forced now, his smile impossibly false. 'Room service,' he said brightly. 'Just a nice quiet evening on the balcony.'

'Anything interesting in your mail?' Her casual enquiry was equally forced as the lift made its way upwards, her tongue sticking to the roof of her mouth as Ciro shook his head and, just as he had when the phone had rung in the middle of the night, he effectively dismissed her.

'It's nothing for you to worry about.'

CHAPTER TEN

'LOOK at you!' Judith's smile was wide as Harriet made her way over to the nurses' station, noticing her colleagues' mostly red faces and averted eyes, except, of course, for Judith, who was making a point of welcoming her, and Charlotte, who was staring at Harriet as if she'd got two heads. Clearly she'd been expecting an emotional wreck to arrive on shift this morning, not the newly tanned, glowing version that was walking towards the nurses' station. 'You should take overdoses more often if that's the effect it has on you!'

'Judith!' Susan nudged her, but Harriet just laughed, more grateful than she could say to Judith for getting the awkward subject out in the open. 'How are you feeling?'

'Great.'

'Well, you certainly look it,' Judith enthused, ready to get on with handover now, shooting a warning look at the gathered nurses, letting them know in no uncertain terms that the subject was most definitely closed. But Charlotte's interest obviously hadn't been quenched quite enough.

'What about Drew? Have you heard from him?'

It was Judith doing the nudging now and Harriet

wished she could force the same bright laugh she had about her supposed overdose, but she couldn't. Drew's infidelity and her impending divorce were way too painful to be relegated to a laughing matter. 'We've spoken,' Harriet said tightly, which was perhaps stretching the truth, but she wasn't going to add 'through our solicitors' to someone as nosy or insensitive as Charlotte.

'Now,' Judith said crisply, her eyes shooting Charlotte a fierce warning look, 'let's get on with work. Harriet, I'd love to ease you in gently, but as you know there's no such thing in this department. Would you mind being in charge of Resus this morning? You've got a couple of other nurses in there with you, and naturally if there's a heavy patient or any lifting you're to leave well alone. I just really need an experienced nurse in there.'

'That's fine.' Harriet smiled, and as easily as that she was back, accepted back into the fold as if she had never been away, the fierce, bitchy, protective arms of Emergency wrapping around her.

'No major changes that I can think of while you've been away.' Judith screwed up her forehead in concentration. 'Except for the roster—oh, and Dr Delgato.' Smiling at Harriet's obvious bemusement, Judith happily continued, 'We've decided he's a honey— finally, a guy who knows how to treat a lady—so we're doing all his blood work for him now and filling in his X-ray slips…'

Harriet gave a low laugh. 'In other words, he's one of us?'

Judith nodded, picking up her clipboard, small talk over and ready to start the shift. 'It's just a shame that he's only temporary!'

Temporary.

That single word was a branding iron to her soul—transient, impermanent, a short-term fix to ease the pain, but over the days and weeks that followed she came to depend upon it more and more.

She woke up each morning to the scent of freshly brewed coffee placed on her bedside table, the one domesticated thing Ciro did. And she adored him for it, adored that tiny loving gesture, dark eyes welcoming her into a new day as he slipped back into bed beside her and made love as only Ciro knew how.

'Let's tell them,' he whispered one morning, when the coffee had long since gone cold, when for the second time in as many days Harriet would have to forgo breakfast if she wanted to get to work on time.

'Tell them what?' Harriet murmured, stretching like a lazy cat, Ciro's hand idly stroking one breast, her mind half-asleep but her body slowly waking under his touch.

'About us,' Ciro whispered. 'I'm fed up hiding it.' His warm breath tickled the tiny hairs on her ears.

But Harriet pulled away, stepping out of bed and calling over her shoulder as she headed for the shower, 'Not yet.'

'Why not yet?' Ciro asked. 'Why can't we tell people?'

The question had merit, but Harriet refused to be lulled back to bed.

'I'm late, Ciro.' Harriet raised her hands, copying one of his exasperated gestures. 'We'll talk about it later.'

'You're doing a double shift today,' Ciro pointed out. 'You're hardly going to be in the mood for talking tonight.'

'Then we can talk about it at the weekend,' Harriet reasoned. 'A few days either way aren't going to make much difference.'

She was actually pleased to be in a rush for once, glad that she had a genuine excuse to avoid this difficult subject, and she could feel Ciro's eyes on hers as she hastily packed her bag and put on a slick of lipstick without the aid of a mirror.

'What are you going to do with your day off?' Harriet asked, not wanting to leave with the atmosphere awkward, but Ciro was sulking, flicking through the newspaper and barely looking up.

'Nothing.' He shrugged. 'Perhaps a walk on the beach later, write a few letters home, I might catch up on some sleep. What time do you finish?'

'Nine, nine-thirty.' Picking up her bag, she gave him a quick kiss before dashing for the door, and even though he kissed her back, smiled and wished her a nice day, Harriet knew he wasn't pleased.

And she couldn't blame him a bit. Time and again he'd tried to broach the difficult subject, time and again she'd avoided it, not quite ready to face the inevitable— just trying to enjoy what little time they had left.

'Damn!' As the hospital loomed Harriet automatically reached for the ID tag around her neck to open the staff car park boom gate. Realising it was missing, she rummaged through her bag on the passenger seat, knowing it was useless. She could almost see it in her mind's eye hanging over the mirror in her bedroom. Glancing down at her watch, Harriet wondered whether to just park in the emergency car park and fumble through the rest of the day without it, but almost immediately she decided against it. A double shift without access to the drug cupboard wasn't particularly appealing.

Executing a rather messy U-turn, Harriet punched in the saved number on her hands-free phone, asking the switchboard operator to put her through to Emergency and apologising profusely to Judith, who naturally was already there and awaiting handover.

'I'll be twenty minutes late,' Harriet said, as Judith's rather resigned sigh filled the car. 'I really am sorry. Is it really busy?'

'Just drive safely,' Judith boomed, not answering Harriet's question. 'The last thing we need is another MVA to add to the list.'

Which did nothing to make her feel better!

The hilly suburbs of Sydney weren't exactly designed for peak-hour traffic and Harriet's twenty minutes were already nearly up as she turned into Beach Street. For speed's sake she decided to forgo the apartments' undercover car park, instead scanning the kerbside for a parking spot—preferably two together, given that she hadn't reverse-parked since her driving test! Finding only one, Harriet attempted the manoeuvre, turning the wheel anticlockwise and reversing slowly, her eyes on the rear-view mirror checking for obstacles. She grew increasingly flustered as an impatient motorist hooted loudly at her rather haphazard attempts and wondered how the hell everyone else seemed to manage to make it look so damned easy.

Checking her rear-view mirror again, her first thought as she saw Ciro striding down the steps at the front of the apartments was that he had come to help, that somehow he'd seen the absolute hash she was making of things.

Her second thought was devastation.

Numb now to the hooting vehicles, the mini traffic jam she had created, Harriet turned her head and looked properly at him, and her third thought hurt even more.

Utterly, utterly beautiful.

Dressed to impress in a stunning grey suit, sunglasses over his eyes, freshly shaven, briefcase in hand, he was jumping into a taxi, impatiently gesturing to the driver and heading in the opposite direction.

'Come on, love, you could get a bus in there.'

She could hear the shouts, the hooting, but she felt numb. Completely on autopilot, she rotated the wheel clockwise, slid the car into the tiny gap and sat there. She willed herself to be calm, convincing herself that there was surely some sort of explanation, that someone must have called him urgently. He was meeting a friend perhaps and when she came home tonight, her mind would be put at rest, she'd laugh at her own insecurity. Just because she'd come home unannounced...

Burying her face in her hands, Harriet let out a low moan, tiny buried thoughts pinging into her consciousness—a hidden letter, middle-of-the-night phone calls, every nurse in the department just a little bit in love with him...

Surely it wasn't happening all over again?

It was possibly the worst double shift of her entire life, the hours dragging on endlessly, the department horribly quiet the one time Harriet wanted it to be furiously busy, just to keep her mind off the endless questions that popped into her head. Time and again she reached for the telephone, wanting to ring to see if Ciro was back, to find out where he'd been. But time and again she pulled back, determined not to go down that road, determined to keep her faith. Just because Drew had cheated, it didn't mean that Ciro was doing the same thing.

'You've got a surprise visitor.' Charlotte knocked on the office door where Harriet was vainly attempting to make use of the quiet evening to fill out some appraisal forms.

The grad nurses were coming towards the end of their allocation and now the senior staff had the difficult task of grading them. For a stupid moment Harriet's heart soared, vainly hoping that it was Ciro, that finally her mind would be put at ease. 'Alyssa Harrison, she's a patient on the adolescent unit. The young anorexic—'

'I remember Alyssa,' Harriet broke in. 'Is she here now?'

Charlotte nodded. 'She was looking for Ciro, but when I told her that he was off today she asked if she could talk to you.'

'That's fine,' Harriet agreed, clicking off her pen and smiling as Alyssa walked in. 'Hi, Alyssa,' Harriet said brightly. 'Come in and have a seat. AU knows that you're down here, I hope?'

'I'm allowed to go for a half-hour walk now.' Alyssa tentatively took a seat. 'So long as I stay in the hospital grounds.'

'You must have been behaving, then! You're certainly looking better than the last time I saw you!'

She was! Even though Alyssa was still painfully thin, that cachectic, gaunt look was mercifully gone, once-sunken eyes sparkling a bit now, and even though there was still an NG tube in place the fact she was being allowed out of the unit for short walks showed that she must be co-operating with her treatment.

'I'm feeling better,' Alyssa admitted. 'It's been hard, though. I'm forty-two kilos now. Three more kilos till I reach my discharge weight and I can finally go home!'

Three kilos maybe didn't sound very much, but Harriet knew that the last couple of kilos were often the hardest to gain and that, despite Alyssa's desire to go home, there would be anxiety about that, too, the outside world a scary place away from the control and counselling in the adolescent unit. The problems Alyssa had faced would still be out there, but hopefully now she'd be armed with strategies to deal with them.

'Well, it's good to see you so well and really nice that you popped down here to see us. Most patients forget about Emergency once they get to the ward.'

'Actually…' Alyssa fiddled with a small paper-weight on Harriet's desk '…I was hoping to see Dr Delgato. He's been coming in to see me on Wednesdays to check how I'm doing. That's my weigh-in day,' Alyssa explained with a note of urgency. 'I really wanted to tell him that I'd finally got to forty-two kilos.'

'Dr Delgato's on a day off, today, Alyssa,' Harriet responded in a matter-of-fact voice, but Alyssa was starting to get teary.

'You see, I lost 200 grams last week. I really wanted to tell him that I've gained…'

'You can tell him when he gets back.'

'Which is when?'

'I'm not sure,' Harriet lied, certainly not about to divulge Ciro's off-duty roster, 'but I'm sure he'll come up and see you when he gets a chance. I know that Dr Delgato likes to keep an eye on patients, and if he said he'd be coming back to see you then he will.' Glancing at her watch, Harriet gave a small grimace. 'I really do need to get on, Alyssa, and I would think your half-hour's probably almost up.'

If she sounded a little bit harsh, it wasn't accidental. As much as she liked Alyssa, as much as she wanted to help, she simply didn't have the skills or time to help adequately, and getting involved, only to pull back, could do more damage than good.

'Damn you, Ciro!' The words whistled out of her

mouth as the office door closed, furious with him for letting Alyssa down.

'You didn't come up?' Ciro gave her a quizzical smile as he came into her apartment. 'I thought we could ring for Chinese—'

'I ate at work.' Flustered, Harriet busied herself wiping down her kitchen bench, which was a pretty futile exercise given that she'd only been in for half an hour and the apartment had been serviced that day. 'It was pretty quiet this evening so we rang for a pizza. You get some, though.'

'I'm fine.' He was frowning slightly, clearly bemused that she hadn't come up to his apartment or at least buzzed to say that she was back. 'Do you want a drink or anything?'

'No, thanks.' Harriet shook her head and, turning her back to him, ran a cloth over the spotless sink as she struggled desperately to keep her voice light. 'How was your day?'

'Nice.'

'What did you do?'

'Nothing much.'

'You didn't go out?'

'No.'

'It's just…' Turning, she forced herself to face him, but with a sinking feeling she already knew that he was lying. She registered the tiny nervous dart of his eyes and could hear the defensive note in his voice as he turned it all on her.

'Harriet, what is this? I told you this morning I was just going to write a few letters, walk on the beach. Did you ring or something and I wasn't home?'

'No!'

'Because I had a sleep. I was tired…'

Harriet nodded, blinking back tears, absolutely refusing to cry, scarcely able to believe that he could look at her and lie, that the man she trusted, the man she adored, the one person who really knew how bad it had been for her, could put her through it all over again.

'I saw Alyssa today,' Harriet said with a definite edge to her voice. 'She was a bit upset that you hadn't been up to the adolescent unit.'

'Ah, Alyssa!' Ciro closed his eyes briefly and nodded.

'Apparently for the last few weeks you've been coming to see her on Wednesdays—the day she gets weighed,' she added. When Ciro didn't respond, Harriet carried on talking. 'She wanted to tell you herself that she'd gained some weight.'

'That's good.' Ciro's eyes narrowed at the brittle edge to Harriet's voice.

'She was *quite* upset actually.'

'It was my day off,' Ciro pointed out. 'My first day off in a fortnight. Did you explain that to her?'

'I did, but shouldn't you have done that, Ciro?' Her eyes were accusing. 'If you always go in on a Wednesday, then you'd surely know that Alyssa would have been waiting for you, would have spent the entire day worrying when you didn't show up.' She heard him suck in his breath in irritation, but ignored it. The anger that had simmered unchecked all day finally had an out, and she used it.

'You shouldn't make promises you can't keep. You shouldn't tell someone that you're going to be there for them if you're not prepared to see it through. I know that you probably meant well and that at the start your intentions would have been good. I can even understand how tempting it would have been to get her to agree to admission and treatment by telling her that you'd follow her progress. But if you weren't prepared to see it through, you shouldn't have started it. How hard would it have been to tell her that you were off on Wednesday this week? You, better than anyone, know how dependent these types of patients can get.'

'I also know—better than anyone,' he added with a distinct edge to his voice, 'how manipulative *these* types of patients can get. I haven't been to see Alyssa every Wednesday, actually. I drop by once a week, and as it turns out the last time was on a Wednesday.'

'Oh.' Suddenly the high moral ground Harriet had been standing on wasn't quite so steady any more, and it slipped even further as Ciro tersely continued.

'I spoke to her case worker on Monday and we decided that I should start stretching out my visits, that this week it would be on Thursday, next week it would be on Friday and the following week I was to miss visiting Alyssa altogether.' He stared at her for the longest time. 'You're right, Harriet. That first night, when Alyssa was scared and confused and had no one, not even her mother, on her side, it was very easy to make promises, but not one of them did I make lightly. My own sister probably owes her life to a nurse in an emergency unit in America who somehow connected with her, who somehow managed to reach out to her and persuade her to take the help that was on offer. Maybe I am helping Alyssa for the wrong reasons, maybe I am somehow attempting to repay some imaginary debt, but do not stand there and accuse me of *forgetting* about my patients or being—'

'I'm sorry.' She halted him with her apology. 'I should have known you wouldn't have let her down without good reason.'

'What's wrong, Harriet?' As direct as ever, Ciro got straight to the point. Harriet knew he probably didn't understand what had happened, couldn't fathom why she just wasn't falling into his arms as she usually did. 'This isn't just about Alyssa, is it?'

And he was right. The problem wasn't, and never had been, Alyssa. The problem was right here in the room and, like it or not, she had to face it. Running a tongue over her dry lips, she forced herself to face him, to answer the question in his eyes with one of her own.

'What is it you've been trying to tell me these last few weeks, Ciro?'

'Harriet.' Ciro shook his head. 'It's late, you're tired and upset. Now really isn't the time—'

'Oh, but it is.' Bravely she looked at him, gave a tiny nod to tell him that whatever he had to say she was now ready to hear it. 'You said something about us being in different places right now?'

'Yes.' It was Ciro raking his hand through his hair now, Ciro the nervous one, Ciro looking anywhere other than at her. 'I never expected things to happen so quickly between us. When we kissed, I said at the time we should take things slowly. There were so many things we should have sorted out before…' His voice trailed off and Harriet spoke for him.

'And we probably would have…' Harriet gave a very faint smile '…if some teenager hadn't decided to go skinny-dipping. Tell me, Ciro,' she urged softly, even though she didn't want him to, even though she didn't want to hear what she was sure was about to be said, hoping against faint hope that she'd got things wrong, that somehow she'd misread the huge writing that had been scrawled on the wall long before they'd even started. But as soon as he started talking Harriet's worst fears were realised and, however expected, however gently spoken, each word was like a brutal slap to her paling cheeks.

She could see the flash of tears in his dark eyes yet, unlike Drew's farewell speech, Harriet knew that Ciro wasn't acting, knew that this was hurting him, too. 'When I came to Australia I never expected anything like this to happen…'

'But it did.' Tears were falling now, thick, salty tears that stung as they rolled down her cheeks, and Harriet didn't even bother to wipe them away.

'I'm just not sure that I'm ready to settle down, Harriet. There are too many…' He didn't finish. His future dreams the very last thing she wanted or needed to hear right now.

'Ciro.' Clearing her throat, Harriet stared at him for an age before talking, somehow trying to capture that last moment in the dying stages of a relationship when it was all still just about them, tracing every delicious feature on the pages of her memory, staring deep into those dark mocha pools one final time while she still had the right to, enough intimacy still there to allow for that tiny indulgence. 'It's OK.' Somehow she managed a wobbly smile, somehow she managed to smile through her tears, but Ciro knew her too well to be fooled.

'Don't try and pretend you're OK, Harriet…'

She couldn't take his sympathy.

'Ciro.' She said his name more clearly now, wiped the back of her cheeks with her hands and, as she'd so recently predicted, failed now to look him in the eye. 'I've just come out of a long and difficult relationship. I've just had the demise of my marriage reported in the newspaper, passed around the hospital grapevine like a sordid game of Chinese whispers.'

'Chinese whispers?'

She didn't even try to explain that one! Instead, Harriet scraped together every last bit of dignity she could muster, stood five feet three proud inches tall and even managed a smile. 'If I can deal with that, I'm sure I can cope with the end of an extended holiday romance. It's been nice.'

'Nice?'

'It's been wonderful.' Harriet swallowed hard. 'It was everything I needed at the time, Ciro. But now it's over.'

'And you're OK with that?' Clearly a man as divine as Ciro wasn't quite used to a woman taking things so well. Bemusement etched his face, his voice aghast when he spoke. 'Just like that, you want to finish!' He stared at her as if he didn't even recognise her.

'As you said before, when it's over it's over.' She dusted her hands together just as he had done, wincing inside as he walked towards her because if he touched her she knew she would dissolve, that the bravado would disappear like a puff of smoke. 'You'd better go.'

'Surely we should talk.'

'There's nothing left to say.' Her eyes, her stance thankfully stopped his progress, gave her enough room to see it through. 'It's been a long day, Ciro. I'm tired, and I just want to go to bed. Alone,' she added. 'This is one book you won't be taking down and reading again.'

'Harriet, please!' Ciro's voice was hoarse. 'Can we at least—?'

'Be friends?' Harriet finished the question for him with a shake of her head. 'Let's just settle for civil for now, shall we?'

And as Ciro walked out of her door, Harriet raised an imaginary glass, managed one final act of bravado before the world seemed to crash down around her.

CHAPTER ELEVEN

'YOU'D never relax, would you?'

Checking the resus equipment was a boring but necessary job, but Charlotte's incessant chatter was already seriously getting on Harriet's nerves and the massive clock on the wall hadn't even got to eight a.m. yet!

'I mean, with someone so divine you'd always know there was fierce competition. Every time you had a row, you'd know there were a zillion women waiting to step in and sympathise.'

'Charlotte,' Harriet said through gritted teeth, 'a relationship isn't supposed to be a competition. It's not about looking fabulous all the time just to keep a man happy, or not daring speaking your mind just so you don't upset him and he rushes off to someone else! It's supposed to be a partnership, an equal, loving partnership. Now, can we please stop talking about Drew and get on with checking the equipment?'

'But I wasn't talking about Drew!' Charlotte responded, apparently horrified at the mere suggestion. 'I'm not that insensitive, Harriet. Goodness, what do you take me for? I was talking about Dr Drop-Dead-Gorgeous Delgato.'

'Oh.'

'Flirting with all the nurses.'

'Oh!' Harriet swallowed hard, suddenly wishing that they *were* talking about Drew.

It had been a full week since she and Ciro had broken up.

The longest, most painful week of her life.

Even in her spite, even in her desolation, the brave words she'd said to Ciro had made sense at the time. Harriet had even faintly believed them. She'd survived the break-up with Drew—surely she could deal with this!

Only in practice it hadn't been so easy.

Working alongside him, seeing him each day, talking with him, discussing patients, even hearing the latest Ciro Delgato gossip, was proving a slow painful torture and yet, in a perverse, maudlin way, she was growing to depend on it. But for how much longer?

The question that everyone in the department was asking right now filled Harriet with dread as the answer became clearer.

Ciro was preparing to move on, the whispers about him leaving growing louder by the day. The three-month assignment might apparently be too much of a commitment for a guy like Ciro. Her fears were further confirmed as Charlotte chatted on.

'But not for much longer, though,' Charlotte whispered theatrically, restocking the ET tubes in the wrong order and not even attempting to put things right as Harriet pointedly pulled them all down and proceeded to replace them correctly. Harriet felt her heart plummet further, if that were possible. 'According to my friend Becky in Admin, he isn't even going to see out this month—he's already handed in his notice and he's only going to give them a week. He's going back to Spain.'

'Charlotte.' Harriet's voice was unusually sharp. 'In

case you haven't noticed, this is a resuscitation room, not the staff social club or the locker room. And if your friend Becky wants to keep her job I suggest she learns to be more discreet. How dare she disclose something so personal?'

'She only told me—' Charlotte attempted, but Harriet had heard enough.

'Quite, which is tantamount to walking around the department with a megaphone! Now, instead of worrying about how you're going deal with Dr Delgato's sudden departure, I suggest that you expend your mental energy on the rather more relevant task of ensuring the equipment is all in order.'

'I was,' Charlotte protested, colouring. 'I can talk and work at the same time.'

'Oh, you can talk,' Harriet retorted, then checked herself, realising that, however upset she was at Charlotte's remarks, her anger was misdirected. 'Just check these ET tubes properly, please. They need to be in order of size. There isn't time to fumble around trying to find the right sized tube when the anaesthetist is calling for it to intubate someone.'

Aware of Charlotte's eyes constantly on her, it came almost as a relief when the department picked up, the occasional dribble of ambulances and walking wounded soon replaced with a constant procession. More than a few found their way into Resus. But, annoying as Charlotte could be, she had all the makings of being a very good emergency nurse. Her sharp eyes picked up even the most subtle of grimaces, her effortless chatter put even the most anxious patients at ease and, most importantly of all, when she wasn't sure of something she wasn't too proud to ask for advice. As Resus steadily filled, Harriet was glad to have her on board.

'How's it going?' Judith popped her head in, groaning at the sight of full trolleys as Harriet pulled up a vial of Valium. 'Do you need me to send someone in to help?'

'If you can spare someone.' Harriet nodded.

Which meant 'Yes, please'!

'I'll see what I can do, but we've just had three in from a motor vehicle accident. It wasn't high impact,' Judith quickly assured her as Harriet's eyes widened in concern. 'We didn't even get an alert from Ambulance Control. But one of the patients has developed severe abdo pain since she arrived. Ciro's in with her now. I just thought I should let you know in case you need to make some space.'

'Charlotte's just about to take that MI to the ward,' Harriet said, 'so if you need to, you can bring her over now.'

'Since when did I need an invitation?' Judith laughed, making to go, but Harriet called her back.

'Can you just check this Valium with me?' Harriet asked. 'It will save me calling Charlotte out. The sooner she gets that patient to CCU the better.'

'Sure.' Pulling on her glasses, Judith checked the vial against the scribble that passed for a prescription on the casualty card. 'How's she doing?'

'Not great,' Harriet answered. 'She came in convulsing, with a temp of 40.3, and we haven't got it down yet. Paeds are in with her now so I'm pulling this up just in case she starts having seizures again.'

'I meant Charlotte,' Judith said, lowering her voice and signalling for Harriet to come closer. 'I've got to do her appraisal this afternoon. She's applied for one of the permanent RN positions now that her grad year's nearly up, and I have to admit I'm stumped. I just don't know what way to go with Charlotte. How have you found her?'

'Good,' Harriet said tersely, tapping the bubbles out of the syringe as Charlotte wheeled the patient out of the resus doors, chatting away to the concerned wife as if they were old friends yet keeping one beady eye on the cardiac monitor on the patient's gurney. 'She's on the ball, her knowledge is great, and she knows when she's out of her depth—'

'I know all that,' Judith answered, irritated. 'I'm asking for your opinion on Charlotte. How do you think she'd do down here as a permanent member of staff?'

'It's not my call,' Harriet answered, but it didn't appease Judith for a moment.

'If you're going to be ANUM, this is the type of decision you'll be making, so stop sitting on the fence and tell me what you think, Harriet.'

So she did. Pushing personal feelings aside, Harriet pondered the issue for a moment and, though it galled her to admit it, she finally gave a tight shrug. 'She'll make a great emergency nurse.'

Judith gave a low laugh. 'You mean she's an utter bitch!'

'Judith?'

Two syllables, but somehow Ciro managed to make them sound sexy, and even though Harriet had seen him on and off all morning, just the sight of him walking over, tired and a little ragged, scratching his head as he held out a casualty card, had Harriet's heart tripping over itself. Her cheeks positively flamed, and she wished he didn't trigger such a violent reaction in her, that she could be one of those women who somehow managed to deliver a cool, vague greeting even if they were dying inside.

'What can I do you for?' Judith smiled, a stark contrast to the angry woman Harriet had seen on Ciro's first night on duty, clearly yet another female who had succumbed to his undeniable charms! 'How's young Pippa doing?'

'Not so good.' Ciro shook his head, his expression serious.

'Do you want to bring her over?' Judith asked, but Ciro declined.

'I want to speak with you both.' As Harriet opened her mouth to question him he got there first. 'Simple MVA, she was a rear-seat passenger and initially presented as a possible seat-belt injury. However, she developed abdo pain on arrival. I've done a brief examination and she's pregnant.'

'She's fifteen years old,' Judith barked and Ciro raised his hands in an elaborate 'not my fault' gesture.

'That's right, Judith. And not only is Pippa pregnant, she is also insisting that she is a virgin, that there is no way she could possibly be pregnant. She's absolutely terrified…'

'How far along do you think she is?' Harriet asked, her own feelings of discomfort around Ciro firmly pushed aside. The patient was the priority now.

'She won't let me formally examine her, but I briefly felt her stomach and I would put her at thirty, maybe thirty-two weeks. She is contracting…'

'She'll have to go to the maternity department,' Judith started, but Ciro put his hand up to halt her.

'This girl may have internal injuries from the accident—there is no way I am going to transfer her. The maternity department can send down a team if she is about to deliver, but until I examine her I won't know how far along she is. We might even be able to stop the labour. Right now my main concern is convincing this very scared young girl that she really is in labour and about to have a baby.'

'You'd probably do better with her.' Judith looked over at Harriet. 'A labour I can deal with blindfolded, but I'm not exactly the world's most patient person.'

'I'd never have guessed!' Ciro teased, but he gave Judith a very grateful smile, no doubt pushing his own personal feelings aside in the name of patient care. Harriet was definitely the best person for the job. 'So, can I take Harriet?'

'For now,' Judith agreed. 'Do you want me to call the maternity department, tell them to have a team on standby?'

'Please.' Ciro nodded. 'Her mother is in cubicle two with a nasty laceration to her forehead, and the father is out in the waiting room ringing relatives. Keep them out of the way of Pippa for now.'

'I suppose you want me to talk to them?'

'You are so strict.' Ciro somehow made it sound like a compliment. 'So very matter-of-fact. I think it would be better if they heard it from you—naturally not until I have properly examined Pippa and hopefully have her consent. But before that, get me the obstetrician on call. If her labour's not that advanced, hopefully we can stop it.'

'Right.' Judith pulled out the hands-free phone from her tabard. 'But if there's any chance of her delivering soon, I want her brought straight over here. I'll set up the paediatric resus cot just in case…'

A wail from resus two halted the conversation. As Harriet had predicted, the febrile child was having another seizure and Judith took the vial of Valium from Harriet, calling out to Susan to come in to Resus and assist, the already busy department stepping up a notch. 'Keep me up to date,' she called, and Harriet nodded, grabbing an emergency delivery pack from the resus shelves and hoping it wouldn't be needed.

Pippa was very young, very scared and, as Harriet quickly realised, very much in active labour!

'She's moved along quickly,' Ciro said almost as soon as he stepped inside.

'Pippa, my name's Harriet,' she introduced herself as she walked in, taking in the dark hair plastered to the girl's head and the terrified eyes in her chubby face as Pippa attempted to climb down from the trolley. 'Dr Delgato said that—'

Harriet didn't even get to finish the sentence as a guttural groan escaped the young girl's lips as she stilled for a moment, her hands fiercely clutching the side of the trolley. Harriet put her arm around the tense shoulders. Glancing down at her watch, she placed her other hand on Pippa's stomach, timing the length and strength of the contraction as she watched the young girl's toes literally curling in pain. Harriet knew that the gentle speech she had mentally rehearsed on her brisk walk over to the cubicle was already past its use-by date, that the restlessness and agitation wasn't just down to denial and fear, but because Pippa was in transition, the first stage of labour over, her body ready to push.

'Pippa.' Harriet's voice was gentle but firm as the contraction ended, and she deliberately stared into the young girl's eyes as she spoke. 'You're having contractions—'

'No!'

'Yes!' Harriet said immediately. 'Yes,' she said again, only more slowly this time, nodding her head as she did so. Thankfully this time Pippa didn't argue. 'Dr Delgato *has* to examine you now. We need to see how far along you are and how the baby's doing.'

'I can't be having a baby,' Pippa wailed, starting to panic all over again. 'I've never even—'

'Yes, Pippa, you have,' Harriet said firmly, absolutely refusing to be drawn into a pointless argument when there simply wasn't time. Ciro had placed a Doppler on Pippa's stomach, a tiny microphone that amplified the baby's heartbeat, and Harriet could hear it fast and regular, which was a reassuring sign. 'Do you remember when your last period was? We need to know so we can try to work out how far along your pregnancy is.'

'We were just messing,' Pippa sobbed. 'It was only the once.'

'When? Pippa, I'm just going to examine you. I will be as gentle as I can.' Ciro was peeling back the blanket as Harriet took over holding the Doppler. Time really was of the essence. 'When did you have intercourse? Do you remember the date?'

'No!' A scream escaped her lips as Ciro attempted to examine her, sheer fear taking over.

'Pippa.' Ciro took a moment, which perhaps they didn't have, but reassuring this terrified young woman was the absolute priority. Without her trust, without her on side, the entire process would be made all the more traumatic, not just for Pippa but possibly for her baby.

'Pippa.' Walking to the top end of the bed, he lifted her chin, forcing the young girl to look at him. 'I am a doctor. My only concern is your health and that of your baby…' He let the word sink in, then elaborated further. 'You *are* having a baby, and, from what I can see, the baby is very small. Now, I need to examine you to see how far along your labour is.' She didn't answer but at least now Pippa wasn't refusing. She appeared to actually be listening. 'I know this is very scary for you, that you are worried about so many things…'

'My parents…'

'Your parents are being looked after, they are not going to come in just yet. If it makes things easier, we will speak to your parents for you.'

'No!'

'They have to know, Pippa.' Ciro's voice was very firm. 'This is not going to go away by just pretending it isn't happening. It *is* happening and we have to deal with it. For now I am asking you to trust me, to try and not worry about your parents or anything that is scaring you. Right now you need only to concentrate on what Harriet or I are saying. Everything else we can deal with later.'

There was something immeasurably reassuring about Ciro, Harriet realised as he spoke to Pippa. For all the jokes among the nursing staff that finally there was a man who knew what women wanted, they were actually speaking the truth. Ciro had an elusive skill he had somehow perfected, reaching out to his patient and somehow establishing trust, somehow managing to throw out the superfluous and get straight to what mattered. Harriet remembered how scared and alone she had felt the night she had been brought into Emergency. Remembered, perhaps for the first time, just how utterly wretched she had felt that night. Yet somehow Ciro had reached her, somehow in the most trying of circumstances he had offered her a mental hand to hold and she had grasped it. And Pippa was doing the same.

'Easter! It was the Easter holiday...' she attempted as Ciro examined her, but there was no other information forthcoming as another contraction hit.

'She's fully dilated.'

Pippa was groaning loudly now, and Harriet rummaged in her pocket and handed him a daisy

wheel—a small cardboard chart that enabled a swift cal-
culation of dates. The Doppler was still picking up the
baby's heartbeat but the dip in the heart rate during the
contraction and the relatively long delay in it picking
up afterwards was extremely concerning—an ominous
sign that the baby was in distress and needed to be delivered soon.

Ciro's voice was calm but his eyes were worried as
they met Harriet's.

'Thirty-one—maybe thirty-two weeks.' Ciro fiddled
with the cardboard.

'Let's get her over,' Harriet started, but that tiny
window of opportunity closed. Pippa was bearing down
now and Ciro was peeling back the blanket and simultaneously reaching for the glove box.

'Let's not,' he said dryly, as Harriet hit the red button
and swiftly opened the delivery pack, pulling on her own
gloves as Judith's concerned face appeared in the
cubicle.

'Can we have the cot in here, please?' Harriet gave
Judith a wide-eyed look. 'Tell the maternity department
it's a thirty-one-weeker and to send the team down
now!'

'Done!' Judith said efficiently, and Harriet knew,
without Judith having to elaborate, that not only would
the maternity department be informed but the anaesthetist and paediatricians, too. Controlled chaos would be
breaking out on the other side of the curtains as the
emergency department rapidly prepared for their
surprise patient—coming, ready or not!

Small babies often came fast, but to prevent any head
trauma the birth needed to be controlled and required
the mother's co-operation. Pippa had clearly had no antenatal care and the baby was premature, which was far

from ideal. But far from ideal was the norm in Emergency—the staff ready and able to deal with whatever was thrown at them, to hopefully make the best out of the worst of circumstances.

'Meconium-stained liquor,' Ciro called as Charlotte came in.

Thankfully, without having to be asked to, she set about doing an essential but not particularly exciting job—pulling chairs and trolleys out of the rather small cubicle to make room for the resus equipment and the staff that would soon be arriving.

'Pippa.' Pulling on a gown, Ciro spoke to his patient as the cot was wheeled in and staff started to arrive. 'There are going to be a lot of people rushing in, a lot of activity, but I want you to listen only to Harriet and me. Just concentrate on what we are telling you to do.'

'I want to push!' Pippa begged, as Judith whispered something to Ciro.

'Gently, then,' Ciro said as Harriet pulled up her knees. 'You hold on behind your knees and give a push, right down into your bottom.'

His expression was one of pure concentration, and he was seemingly oblivious to all the activity taking place in the tiny cubicle around him. The anaesthetist was setting up the resus trolley, unwrapping equipment and connecting a tiny ambu-bag to oxygen. Judith was turning up the heater and pulling up drugs. Ciro's mouth was set in a grim line as he guided the tiny head and Harriet watched closely, watched every flicker of Ciro's reaction, so she could relay what was required back to Pippa.

'Enough,' Ciro said, a frown on his face; the baby's head almost out of the birth canal.

'OK, stop pushing, Pippa,' Harriet said, firmly keeping a lid on her own flutter of fear, something in

Ciro's expression telling her that things weren't right. 'Just pant.'

'The cord's wrapped tightly around the neck.' His eyes locked with Harriet's for a brief second, conveying the urgency of the situation, and she gave an understanding nod as Pippa bore down again.

'Don't push,' Harriet said firmly, because every push was causing the cord to tighten and Ciro needed time to clamp and cut it.

'I have to.'

'You mustn't.' Out of the corner of her eye Harriet could see Judith passing Ciro the clamps, but she looked away. Everything possible was being done and she had to focus solely on Pippa, stop her from pushing to give Ciro the time to clamp and cut the cord. She chose her words carefully, aware that Pippa had had no antenatal education and might not understand about the umbilical cord. 'Your baby's in trouble. We need you to stop pushing. Breathe over it, Pippa.' Harriet's voice was urgent. 'I know it's hard, but you have to pant—you mustn't push.'

'Got it.' Ciro was clearing the baby's mouth and nose with a suction bulb now, removing as much as he could of the thick meconium before the baby took its first breath. 'OK, Pippa,' he called. 'With the next contraction you can push! Give me your hand.'

Harriet guided Pippa's hand down, Ciro realising, no doubt, that because of the denial Pippa had been in and the sheer speed of her labour, she needed this moment to acknowledge that her baby was coming out, needed to feel like an active participant before everyone else took over.

'Good girl.' Ciro's voice was encouraging, jubilant almost, Spanish creeping in as the sheer emotion of the moment started to hit. Harriet could feel tears stinging her eyes as she watched; a privileged spectator as a new life came into the world. '*Buena*, Pippa. Come on, reach down for your *bebé*, lift your baby out with me…'

And despite the dire circumstances somehow he made it beautiful, somehow he made it about Pippa and her baby, not an unexpected premature delivery in a shabby emergency cubicle. Ciro placed the tiny baby into the waiting hands of the paediatrician, who whisked the limp infant to the resus cot.

'You have a son.' Ciro spoke over the noise. 'You did an amazing job, Pippa.'

'Why isn't he crying?'

'The doctors are with him, Pippa,' Harriet answered as Ciro made his way to the cot, observing the activity around the infant. Although Harriet badly wanted to go over to see how the babe was, it was her job to stay with Pippa, to build on the relationship they had forged through the tumultuous delivery and comfort her now as the team worked on. 'They're looking after him.'

Glancing over, Harriet peered through a gap in the throng, her heart in her mouth as she glimpsed the tiny motionless body, the anaesthetist deeply suctioning the babe then placing the ambu-bag over his slack mouth and gently squeezing oxygen into his lungs. It was probably only a matter of seconds but it felt like for ever, time dragging endlessly as Harriet squeezed Pippa's hands. But as she saw a little foot suddenly flex, his body pinking up before her eyes, Harriet squeezed Pippa's hands harder in excitement as a tiny, angry wail filled the cubicle and relief washed over her.

'There he goes,' Harriet said, as if it had been a forgone conclusion that he would, as if she hadn't been holding her breath since the tiny bundle had been delivered. Her eyes locked with Ciro's, the dark mocha pools holding hers, that tiny tired smile on his lips, the tension seeping out of his face as the baby's cry filled the air, replaced quickly with an almost immeasurable look of sadness as he dragged his eyes away. Harriet knew there and then why she was hurting so much, knew in that instant why Ciro's leaving cut far deeper than Drew's infidelity.

With her and Drew it had been over for ages.

With Ciro it had barely even started. Those tiny seeds of emotion he had delicately planted were unfurling unaided now, stretching out like petals towards the sun, the feelings Harriet had for him somehow thriving without sustenance, that chain reaction he had instigated still rolling on. Finally Harriet admitted to herself what deep down she'd probably known for a while.

She loved him.

CHAPTER TWELVE

'HOW could you not know?' Charlotte scoffed disbeliev-ingly as she walked into the staffroom, and even though it was now lunchtime and a couple of hours after the event everyone knew what she was talking about. 'I mean, how could you possibly not know that you were pregnant?'

'How did the parents not know?' Judith huffed, spooning sugar into her coffee and tutting loudly as she did so. 'That's what I'd like to find out.'

'She's quite a big girl,' Harriet said, acutely aware of Ciro sitting on the sofa opposite her and trying des-perately to focus on the conversation instead of him. 'I wouldn't have noticed it without feeling her stomach. I'd have just thought she was overweight.'

'And then she tried to say that she was a virgin!' Judith said again to anyone who cared to listen, ignoring the offered explanation, and Harriet bit down hard on her lip, already sick of the subject that was on everyone's lips. From Ciro's drawn-out sigh he was feeling the same.

'People have an amazing ability to…' he gestured in the air '…*compartimientos*.'

'To what?' Charlotte asked rudely.

'To block things out,' Harriet explained, with as much patience as she could muster through gritted teeth.

'Pippa was obviously terrified of her parents finding out that she'd had sex, let alone the fact she was pregnant, so she just blocked it out, refused to acknowledge it, just hoping it would go away.' As Charlotte rolled her eyes Harriet felt her temper flare. 'Can't you show a bit more compassion? The poor kid made a mistake.'

'Exactly,' Judith sniffed. 'She's a kid, she should never have been messing around in the first place. Once is all it takes...'

Some rapid Spanish was being mumbled from across the room and, judging by the rather strong sentiment behind the words, Harriet wasn't sure it was particularly complimentary. But Judith and Charlotte were too deep in their own gossip to notice, barely even looking up as Ciro stood up and stormed out of the room. Harriet sat for a full two minutes before plucking up the courage to go after him.

Needing to hear for herself if what everyone was saying was true, she finally caught up with Ciro in the ambulance bay outside Emergency, where he stood leaning against the wall, moodily staring out into the distance.

'You know what Emergency can be like,' Harriet said, making her way over. 'I'm sure it's the same in Spain, the same the world over probably! They're just letting off steam in the staffroom.'

'That kid is fifteen years old,' Ciro retorted angrily. 'She did so well today.'

'She was great,' Harriet agreed, but Ciro wasn't about to be soothed.

'And she doesn't deserve being spoken about like that by some nurse who'd drop her knickers if I crooked my finger.'

'Ciro!'

'She would,' Ciro retorted. 'She rings me at home,

asking if I want to come out to some club, asking if I want to meet for drinks, asking if I want to come over… I don't even want to know how she got my number.'

'She rang you at home?' Harriet checked, appalled for Ciro and furious with Charlotte. It had nothing to do with jealousy—emergency staff's telephone numbers were kept in a folder solely in case they needed to be called in urgently—the fact Charlotte had abused the system was enough on its own! 'I'll speak to her this afternoon!'

'I've dealt with it,' Ciro barked, but Harriet shook her head.

'No, Judith needs to know what's happened, Ciro. That folder will have to be locked away if staff are going to use it in such a manner.'

He gave a reluctant nod.

'And then there's Judith.' Reverting back to the earlier topic, clearly Ciro hadn't regretted a word he'd said earlier because his tongue was just as deadly. 'What would she know about birth control?'

'Just because she's not married, Ciro, it doesn't mean that she's never had a relationship. To insinuate that she's frigid—'

'Oh, Harriet,' Ciro scoffed. 'She's not a frigid spinster, she's in a relationship. Her partner's still in the military, waiting for *her* pension.'

'What?' Wide eyes blinked back at him. 'How on earth would you know that?'

'Because…' He gave a helpless shrug. 'She told me.'

'Told you?'

'Yes, Harriet.' Ciro gave a small reluctant grin at Harriet's obvious shock, finally calming down a fraction and letting out a long drawn-out sigh, but he said nothing to put her at ease, made no attempt at small talk, just stared moodily out across the ambulance bay.

It was left to Harriet to fill the uncomfortable silence, trying to find the courage to ask the most difficult question of her life.

'You're leaving?'

He nodded but didn't elaborate.

'Charlotte said you weren't even going to see out the month.'

'It must be true, then!' Sarcasm dripped from every word, but finally he calmed down, dragging his eyes to look at her. 'At the end of the week.'

'It's not…' Harriet swallowed hard. 'I know that things have been a bit uncomfortable between us these past few days…'

'It has nothing to do with us,' Ciro said, and maybe he meant it kindly but it only made Harriet feel worse. 'So don't worry.'

'I'm not.'

'You're sure?' She was turning to go, to head back into the department, but something in his voice made her turn around. 'You're quite sure that there's nothing worrying you, Harriet?'

'What's your problem, Ciro?' Angrily she confronted him. 'I'm trying to be civil here. I came out here to check that you were OK and all you've done is be rude. It's not my fault you're leaving, it's not my fault Judith and Charlotte have upset you…'

'It's not them, it's not even you.' He dragged in some air as Harriet stared at him. 'I'm angry with myself, OK?' Finally he looked at her. 'All I've heard since Pippa delivered and things calmed down is, "Once is all it takes".' He mimicked Judith's booming voice.

'That first night…' He swallowed hard. 'I just assumed you were on the Pill.'

'I was. I am. So if that's what's worrying you, please,

don't bother. I'm not going to mess up your travel plans. I've never missed taking it.'

'Never?'

A frown came to her face as he stared back at her. She raked a hand through her hair, as she did when she was nervous, as realisation hit.

'Apart from that one day, when I didn't have my bag, I've only missed it once.'

'Once is all it takes…'

The irony wasn't lost on Harriet.

'I'm not pregnant.' She shook her head firmly, and forced a very brave smile. 'I know I'm not.'

'Harriet, we slept together every night, every day…' He didn't smile back, just stared at her, the question in his eyes demanding honesty. 'I hate to now state what should have been obvious, but in all that time you never had a period.'

'Look…' Her mind flailed for a response. 'Ciro, I can't deal with hypotheses…' She registered his frown, knew she was talking just a bit too fast for him to understand. 'Let's just leave it for now.'

'You mean refuse to talk about it.' Ciro took a deep, angry breath. 'That is what we do best, isn't it? Ignore things and just hope that they will sort themselves out in the end. Pippa had an excuse, Harriet, she is fifteen years old. Fifteen-year-olds ignore things and hope that they will go away.'

'I'm not ignoring anything,' Harriet snarled. 'I told you before we were even lovers, when you were my doctor, that I wasn't very regular.' Her cheeks were flaming now, but with anger not embarrassment. 'Don't worry, Ciro, I'm not going to trap you.'

'Trap me?'

'That's what's worrying you, isn't it?' Harriet flared.

'You're worried that you might be taking home more than a hat with corks and a couple of stuffed koalas from your holiday…'

'You're being ridiculous,' Ciro retorted. 'I am asking you to tell me if there is a problem. I face up to my mistakes, Harriet.' He reached out to grab her hand but she shook it away.

'Don't worry, no *mistake* was made, Ciro…'

'So you're not pregnant?'

'Thanks for that, Doc!' They both jumped as Pippa's father handed Ciro a mobile phone. 'That was very kind of you—I didn't much fancy letting the whole waiting room know what was going on.'

'You've got hold of everyone, Tony?' Ciro checked, but Pippa's father shook his head.

'Not quite. I think I'll be paying the young fella a personal visit to break the news.'

'The baby's father?'

Tony gave a grim nod. 'I was fit to kill him half an hour ago, but I must be going soft. I'm starting to feel a bit sorry for him. Gary's just a kid himself. Fifteen years old and a father—can you imagine?'

'No,' Ciro admitted. 'With the right support they'll be OK, Tony. And I've a feeling they're going to get it— you and your wife have done very well today in the most trying of circumstances.'

'We've no choice, have we, Doc?' Tony sighed. 'Still, Gary's going to have to face up to this mess the same way Pippa has to. They'll be paying for this for the rest of their lives.'

As Tony headed back inside, Harriet went to go, too. But as she turned away Ciro called her back.

'Harriet? We were talking!'

'No, Ciro, we'd finished talking.' Briefly she looked over her shoulder. 'There's nothing for you to worry about.'

CHAPTER THIRTEEN

'I DIDN'T get his number from the folder!' Cheeks flaming, Charlotte was adamant. 'Anyway, I can't believe you're making such a fuss!'

'Oh, this isn't even close to a fuss,' Judith warned her. 'You should count yourself lucky that Sister Farrell insisted that we speak with you first, hear your side of things. Frankly, I'm all for ringing the nursing supervisor and asking you to be moved to one of the wards!'

'What?' Charlotte's voice was incredulous. 'Because of a telephone call?'

'Because of a gross invasion of privacy.' Harriet's voice was a lot calmer than Judith's but there was no mistaking the anger behind it. 'Charlotte, this may seem ridiculous to you, but the fact is, this emergency department runs on trust. Like those of a lot of medical personnel, Dr Delgato's private number isn't listed in the telephone book. The last thing he needs is an angry, upset patient or relative ringing him at two in the morning.'

'But I'm not a patient or relative,' Charlotte retorted.

'No.' Harriet gave her a withering look. 'You're a member of staff and as such we expect you to act accordingly. That means when you take a shine to one of the doctors or are short of a date, you don't use the emergency manual as your personal directory. Had Dr Delgato wanted you to have his number, he would have given it to you.'

'If it's so private, why isn't it locked up?'

'It is now,' Judith barked. 'Thanks to you. So the next time someone rings in sick and we need an immediate replacement, or there's a patient that needs an urgent second opinion or, heaven help us, we have a major incident, we have to find the keys and unlock the blessed thing.'

'Charlotte.' Harriet's voice was far more reasonable. 'I know this sounds like a non-event to you but, as I was saying earlier, this department runs on trust, and that emergency phone book was an extension of that trust. You've abused it.'

'I didn't,' Charlotte insisted, and Judith let out an exasperated sigh.

'You said this morning that you had a friend in Admin,' Harriet started, and Charlotte's eyes widened. Perhaps the seriousness of the situation was starting to hit home.

'It wasn't Becky—you can't blame her for this.' Running a worried hand across her forehead, Charlotte finally admitted the truth. 'OK, I did take his number out of the book. I'm sorry!' she added. Charlotte didn't look quite so bold now, tears sparkling in her eyes. 'I honestly didn't think anything of it at the time. I was on late shift, there were a few of us going on to a club, and I just thought that Ciro might like to see a bit of Sydney night life.'

'And did he?' Judith asked, because, quite simply, Harriet couldn't bring herself to.

'No.'

'And was that the end of it?'

'No.' Tears were falling now and Harriet actually felt sorry for her—just a twenty-one-year-old with a king-sized crush. 'I rang him later that night, after we'd all had a drink.'

'What time?' Judith's voice was like the crack of a whip.

'Two, maybe three in the morning.'

'Any other times?' Harriet asked, remembering the phone ringing the first night they'd made love, and Ciro's annoyance. Her suspicions were confirmed when Charlotte eventually nodded.

'A few.'

'Do you see now that it was an invasion of privacy?' Harriet asked, only more softly now, taking no pleasure from Charlotte's tears, being careful not to humiliate her further. 'If you want to be a part of this team, Charlotte, you have to act more responsibly. You have to show not just the patients but your colleagues, too, that you're completely reliable, that the trust that's placed in you will never be abused. We don't just treat strangers here, Charlotte. Look what happened to me the other week.'

'I never discussed it…' Charlotte started, but her voice petered out as Harriet raised one questioning eyebrow.

'I'm not saying you went to the newspaper or anything, Charlotte. If I thought that, we'd have had this conversation ages ago, probably with your union rep present.' She paused to let it sink in. 'However, you have taken great delight in telling anyone that will listen, even the patients, that you work with Drew Farrell's wife.'

Only when Charlotte nodded did Harriet continue.

'Charlotte, we thrive on gossip in this place, we all love to be the first to know what's going on, but there's a very fine line that cannot be crossed. What happens in this department has to stay within these walls, whether it's something as simple as a doctor's phone number or something as salacious as…' Harriet plucked wildly for an example and chose one close to home. 'A nursing sister who comes home to find her husband in bed with someone else.

'It might be a member of staff or one of their relatives that comes through the doors, or it might be someone famous. Now, that might sound as if it has nothing to do with scribbling down a doctor's telephone number but the fact of the matter is we're privy to a lot of information down here and as much as we gossip between ourselves it cannot and does not go further. It cannot be abused in any way at all, we have to trust each other on that.'

'I understand.' Charlotte sniffed, and something in her voice told Harriet that finally she did. 'What's going to happen to me?'

Harriet looked over at Judith and from the nod she gave, clearly the ball was in Harriet's court.

'Let's just leave it there. Hopefully, you'll think long and hard about what's been said and if not change your ways at least curb them a bit. We're not trying to fashion you into some sort of robot, Charlotte, but working in Emergency isn't just about following a professional code of conduct but a moral one, too.'

'What about my application?' Charlotte's eyes were urgent. 'Will I still be considered for one of the permanent positions?'

That wasn't Harriet's domain and after a moment's pause Judith finally answered, 'We'll just have to wait and see.'

Both women sat in silence until the door closed, and it was Harriet that took up where Charlotte had left off.

'What *about* her application?'

'I'm not sure.' Judith fiddled with the paperwork in front of her. 'She's got all the makings of a great emergency nurse, she's just too bold at times.'

'She's twenty-one,' Harriet pointed out. 'And gorgeous to boot. Hell, I'd have probably lifted his phone number at that age.'

'Would you?' Judith asked dubiously, and Harriet coloured.

'No!' She gave a low laugh. 'But I'd have been very tempted. Come on, Judith, imagine if you were twenty-one and newly qualified and someone as gorgeous as Ciro—'

'He's not my cup of tea.'

If Harriet had been a bit pink before, she was positively flaming now, Ciro's rather surprise revelation suddenly coming to mind. But Judith just looked at her and laughed.

'Have you only just cottoned on?'

Harriet gave a tiny wince as she nodded. 'Just.' Harriet gave a little giggle. 'And, of course, it doesn't matter to me a bit. I'm just going to blush horribly for the next half-hour or so.'

They both fell into silence but it wasn't uncomfortable, the two women thinking long and hard about the young nurse's future.

'Do you think it was Charlotte that let it slip about you and Drew?'

Harriet gave a shrug. 'I've no idea, but I'm sure I was the talk of whatever bar she was in the next night.'

'Then I'll leave the decision as to whether she gets the position to you.'

'But I've only been here a few months, it's not my call.' As Harriet attempted to protest, Judith became more insistent.

'I don't care if you've been here six months or six years, Harriet. You're an emergency nurse as much as I am, and this has possibly affected you the most. I need to know now. Admin want to know today, so they can get the letter of offer out.'

'So Charlotte was one of your choices?'

'She was.' Judith nodded. 'But, as I say, it's up to you.'

And Harriet thought for a good couple of minutes. Her first instinct was to say no, that Charlotte didn't deserve the job, that there were better candidates.

But were there?

'She's got all the makings of a great emergency nurse,' Harriet said finally. 'And I honestly believe that she's had a fright today.'

'Grown up a bit, even?'

Harriet nodded. 'I may live to regret this, but I think she'll be great.'

'So do I,' Judith agreed. 'I think you've made the right choice. Now, I'd better email Admin with our decision, but don't let Charlotte know.' She gave a shrewd wink. 'It might do her good to stew for a while.'

'One of her closest friends works there.' Harriet grinned. 'We might have scared her a bit, but I can guarantee that she'll know she's in before the end of the shift.'

'Speaking of which…' Judith looked up from the computer '…how about we go for a drink? Strictly as friends.' Judith grinned.

And like a reflex action, Harriet blushed. 'I'm sorry. I swear that I'll be back to normal tomorrow,' she said, fanning her flaming cheeks with her hands. 'And there was me feeling sorry for you. You've got the best sex life out of the lot of us.'

'Perhaps.' Judith laughed. 'But I could really use a

drink and a chat tonight. I've had it up to here with stupid young girls getting themselves pregnant and even sillier young nurses falling for a doctor who's clearly just passing through…' Her voice trailed off, her eyes blinking in concern behind her thick glasses as Harriet visibly crumpled, balling her fingers into her eyes in an attempt to hold back the tears. Harriet's lips trembled as Judith shot from her seat and put her arm around her. 'Whatever's wrong?' Her voice was very concerned. 'Harriet, tell me, what on earth's the matter?'

'Nothing!' Harriet attempted, but it changed midway, her voice breaking into a sob, tears coursing down her cheeks. 'Everything…' Harriet stopped trying to hold it all in, her words strangling in her throat as she tried to get them out, scarcely able to believe, even as she said it, that it was her own life she was describing. 'I'm one of the idiots who fell for him.'

'Ciro?' Judith checked, and Harriet gave a pitiful nod. 'You and Ciro?'

'Ciro bloody Delgato can add me to his list of conquests…'

'You're being daft,' Judith chided. 'The fact even I didn't know about it surely shows it meant more than a passing fling. I was just shooting my mouth off before. Ciro's lovely…' Judith's hand tightening on Harriet's shoulder was like opening the floodgates. Tidal waves of emotion flooded in as Harriet finally admitted the appalling truth.

'Those stupid girls getting themselves pregnant that you were talking about…' She couldn't believe she was saying it, couldn't believe that it was actually happening to her. 'Well, I think that I may be one of them.'

CHAPTER FOURTEEN

'I NEVER thought I'd be buying one of these.'

Placing a loaded carrier bag on the kitchen bench, Judith pulled out the offending article then proceeded to unload the rest of her wares, pulling out tissues and folate tablets—and tampons, just in case Harriet was mistaken. It reminded Harriet of Ciro emptying the emergency rations on her kitchen bench before their first night together as a couple, and she promptly burst into tears all over again.

'It's stress,' Judith said wisely as Harriet duly padded off to the bathroom. 'And don't forget that you've had an anaesthetic as well—they can play havoc with your cycle.'

'How long does it take?' Harriet asked Judith, returning with the plastic indicator. She placed it on a magazine on the coffee-table and tried to forget that the blessed thing was there.

'Long enough to open one of these!' Popping the cork on a bottle of champagne, Judith filled up two glasses. 'Come on, Harriet, you're not sunk yet.'

It was the longest two minutes of her life. She sat there, sipping champagne as the minutes ticked away like hours, not sure how she wanted it to turn out. A negative result would be just that: the end of the end. And yet...

Staring over at the white piece of plastic that would determine her fate, despite the appalling circumstances, despite the cards stacked against her, a part of Harriet actually wanted it to be positive. She had a flutter of excitement inside and if there was such a thing as maternal instinct it kicked in then, images of jet-haired mocha-eyed babies flicking into her consciousness, a permanent reminder of all that could have been.

A *mistake* this baby never would be.

'Time's up!' Ever practical, Judith drained her glass before she headed over to the coffee-table. Picking up the plastic indicator, she stared at it for a long time before finally looking at Harriet.

'Congratulations!'

'Well, that's that, then!' Kissing goodbye to those mental images, Harriet raised her glass, but as Judith still stared Harriet's heart seemed to stop beating, the congratulations Judith had offered perhaps not quite the reverse joke Harriet had expected. 'I'm not?'

'Oh, yes, you are.'

And even from the other side of the room, Harriet could see the dark cross in the middle of the indicator, and she stared open-mouthed at a piece of blotting paper that had suddenly changed her world.

'It will be OK!' Judith was trying to comfort her, trying to say the right thing, and somehow managing.

'I know it will,' Harriet gulped.

'Whatever you decide to do, I'll be there.'

And Harriet knew what Judith was offering, but without hesitation she turned it down.

'I'm keeping it, Judith. It has nothing to do with whether it's right or wrong…' Accepting the glass of water Judith had poured, she downed it in one. 'It's just not me.'

'Then Ciro needs to know,' Judith said sensibly, but

Harriet shook her head, appalled at the prospect of telling him yet equally appalled at the prospect of not telling him, of making such a mammoth decision on her own. Because even if Judith was there, even if Judith was being the best a friend could be, at the end of the day it came down to Harriet.

The choices she made in the next few weeks were ones that she and her baby would have to live with for the rest of their lives—which was a sobering thought indeed.

'He might be upset at first, but once he's calmed down—'

'No!' Harriet shook her head, tentatively at first, not a hundred per cent sure of the path she should follow and struggling to keep up with Judith. 'I don't think I'm going to tell him.'

'Oh, Harriet.' Judith shook her head. 'You can't just let him go without knowing.'

'Oh, but I can.'

And as easily as that she decided. She cupped her hand over her stomach and focussed on the life inside her. Ciro was moving on with his life, his notice had already been handed in, and their relationship was definitely over. What good could it possibly do to tell him?

'There's no need for him to know. It's not as if we're going to be working alongside each other—hell, he's heading back to Spain.'

She moved out onto the balcony. It was easier to be outside than in, easier to stand looking out at the sea and inhaling the delicious night air, to watch the waves endlessly rolling in, the stars still shining brightly, as everything in Harriet's universe changed.

'I heard him today, Judith. Heard him tell me that he's prepared to *pay* for his mistakes.'

'You said yourself to young Pippa that the father needed to know,' Judith pointed out wisely. 'I heard you, Harriet, when we were waiting to transfer her. You said that as hard as it might be to tell him, he had a right to know.'

Harriet turned and faced her friend. 'Pippa's fifteen years old, she needs her family, needs all the help she can get, and she needs the father to take whatever responsibility he can. But I'm almost thirty.' Harriet ran a tongue over her dry lips, tasted the salt of the ocean and drew on its strength. 'I've lived through one bad relationship, Judith, and I can think of nothing worse than doing it all over again—Ciro staying with me out of some sense of duty, watching the passion, all the love we had slowly die until neither of us even have the energy to care much when it's over.'

'But you don't *have* to be together,' Judith pointed out. 'Ciro still needs to know.'

'Why?' Harriet didn't even look over, just stared into the darkness, somehow picturing the scene, a horrible future scenario in which she had no desire to partake. 'So that he can send me a cheque every month, or draft a letter through his solicitor to demand that the baby takes Spanish lessons so it's not out of its depth on its annual custody visit? What's that going to achieve?'

'He's its father.'

'A father who doesn't want to settle down.' Harriet couldn't even cry, numb shock setting in now. 'And if I can't have all of him, I don't want the crumbs. Surely you can understand how I feel. Women bring up babies on their own all the time—some even choose from the outset that they're going to be a one-parent family!'

'It doesn't mean that it's easy,' Judith countered. 'And, yes, some women decide that's what they'll do because it's the only way that they can have a baby. But it's different here, Harriet. This isn't some nameless sperm donor, you're talking about a man you've been in a relationship with, a man you maybe even love…'

'I do love him.' Harriet's voice was a strangled whisper, and she buckled as Judith put her arm around her. 'That's why I have to do it this way.'

'To make it easier for Ciro?' Judith asked, for once her voice not judgmental. She was trying hard to understand, but she still didn't quite get it, and Harriet shook her head.

'No, Judith, to make things easier for me.'

CHAPTER FIFTEEN

'*DÓNDE* es el apartmento de Dr Delgato?'

Possibly the most stunning women Harriet had ever seen greeted her in rapid Spanish as, pale-faced and attempting to hold down half a slice of toast, Harriet dashed out of her door in a vain attempt to get to work on time.

Almost as soon as the indicator had turned positive, morning sickness had arrived, and the apartment, along with Harriet, had a permanent scent of bleach, toothpaste and mouthwash, which only served to exacerbate things!

'I look for Dr Delgato,' the dark-haired beauty explained, screwing up her nose as she did so and peering inquisitively over Harriet's shoulder into her apartment. 'He say second door from the lift, so you can tell me where he is. I come straight from *aerpuerto*. I am his sister, Cara.'

The one with the terrible taste in men, Harriet thought dryly, wondering how someone so beautiful could, over and over, get it so terribly wrong! No one had the right to look that good when they'd come straight from the airport. Not even a hint of jet-lag marred Cara's gorgeous features. Her long dark hair rippled down her slender shoulders as if she'd just stepped out of a beauty salon, and her almond-shaped eyes narrowed as she stared at Harriet, her pretty nose sniffing the air. But for all her arrogance, for all her confidence, if it had been a few weeks ago Harriet would have squealed in delight, would have gleefully introduced herself to this ravishing stranger, but, given she'd already been through this scene the previous night with one of his other sisters—Estelle, the studious one— instead, Harriet gestured upwards.

'You're on the wrong floor. Dr Delgato is the next one up.'

'No!' Annoyingly she shook her head.

'Yes,' Harriet responded with more than a hint of irritation. 'As I explained to your sister last night, Dr Delgato lives on the *fifth* floor, second door from the lift. Now, if you'll excuse me, I'm already late.'

'Bloody vultures,' Harriet moaned to herself, grinding the gears all the way to work. She could just imagine them sitting around Ciro's apartment like witches around a cauldron, discussing their brother's latest victim.

Well, a victim she refused to be!

Checking her appearance in the rear-view mirror, unusually for Harriet these days, she added an extra slick of lipstick, utterly determined to impress the interview panel she would be facing that morning. Plagued with guilt for even considering taking on the role, without revealing she was pregnant. Judith had been the one to talk Harriet out of divulging her status—telling her in her usual militant terms that not only didn't she have to divulge her pregnancy in the application process, even if she were nine months gone and in active labour, her condition had no bearing on the selection process.

Nurses got pregnant all the time and, furthermore, as Judith took apparent delight pointing out, in the absence of any child maintenance from a certain completely-in-the-dark doctor, Harriet would be needing the best wage she could possibly muster. With Judith's pep talk ringing in her ears, Harriet managed to get through the interview. Answering each question thoughtfully, she pondered the various scenarios the interview panel tossed at her. Shaking hands at the end, she even indulged in a mental image of herself in the smart red blouses the ANUM wore.

The maternity version, of course!

'What's this?' Screwing up her face, Harriet tried to decipher the appalling scrawl in front of her then, giving in completely, she thrust the casualty card at Ciro, who was working at the nurses' station. 'I can't even make out what it's supposed to be, let alone dispense it.'

Polite attempts at small talk had long since run out— at least on Harriet's part—and by the time they had reached Ciro's last day in the department they were reduced to clipped requests when anyone was present and fractious barbs from Harriet when they were unfortunate enough to find themselves alone.

'Sorry!' Scribbling out his drug order, Ciro rewrote it, still in his unique appalling scribble but at least it was in English this time. 'I wrote the Spanish name for it.'

'Which would be fine,' Harriet mumbled, taking the chart and heading off, 'if we were in Barcelona.'

'A simple mistake,' Ciro retorted. 'I'm sorry my English isn't perfect enough for you!'

'Your English is fine.' Harriet turned, smiling sweetly, but it went nowhere near her eyes. 'And I'll forgive you for your handwriting, given that dyslexia clearly runs in the family.'

'What?'

'Your sisters!' Her fake smile disappeared. 'Clearly they don't know the difference between the numbers four and five.'

'I have no idea what you are talking about, Harriet!' Ciro's voice had an almost weary note to it, as if she were some sort of raving lunatic he was trying to placate.

'Estelle and now Cara have both been to my door, *pretending* they don't know which apartment is yours.'

'I had no idea. They must have got lost...' Ciro put his hand up in apology. 'I am sorry you were disturbed.'

And somehow he managed to turn it all around until Harriet didn't even know what she thought any more. Why would Ciro's sisters be coming to look at her? Why would Ciro's sisters even care about yet another woman whose heart their brother had broken?

'It doesn't matter.' Harriet managed a very small smile. 'I'm sorry I even brought it up.'

'How was your interview?' Ciro asked magnanimously, but Harriet couldn't do it, couldn't even pretend to be polite, couldn't stand and make idle chatter with the man who'd stomped all over her heart. Without answering, she turned and walked away.

'Harriet?' Ciro's voice was a summons but Harriet chose to ignore it.

'I haven't got time to talk,' Harriet called over her shoulder. 'I've got a meeting scheduled in Maternity at three.'

'Maternity?' He was walking alongside her, pushing for more information. 'I'm heading that way, I have to go to Admin to sign some forms. I will walk with you.'

It would have been childish to argue, silly to make a scene, so instead she walked quickly, hating Ciro for trying to be friends.

'I see you are not coming to my leaving do tonight.'

Harriet glared fixedly ahead, didn't even deign to reply. The entire emergency department, it would seem, were heading to Sydney Harbour at the end of Ciro's shift and boarding a boat for a boozy cruise around the harbour. The staff changing room was lined with plastic dry-cleaning bags containing stunning evening dresses, and the usual white shoes that lined the benches were littered now with strappy sandals and make-up bags, curling wands and hair straighteners.

Ciro might have only been in Sydney for a couple of months but there was certainly nothing simple or discreet about his farewell.

The whole department was going to miss him, Harriet most of all, and saying goodbye to Ciro in front of everyone in such a beautiful setting had been enough disincentive for Harriet, not to mention her queasy stomach!

'So what is your meeting about?' Ciro asked when clearly Harriet wasn't going to respond to his first question, but once on the far safer topic of work Harriet cleared her throat and managed to answer, praying the conversation would last long enough to see her to her destination.

'We're just going over Pippa's birth. Even though it went well, it raised a few issues.'

'Such as?'

'Well, we tend to rely on the fact that there's a maternity department in the hospital, but, as Pippa's baby proved, not every mother gets to the labour ward in time. We're just going to go over the equipment that was used and see if we need to update it. We're also going to discuss the possibility of a short rotation through the delivery unit for some of the senior staff—just to keep everyone up to date.'

'Sounds like a good idea. Was it yours?'

'Partly,' Harriet admitted modestly.

'Quite the upcoming ANUM,' Ciro responded with a tight smile. 'I'm sure you'll do very well.'

'Thank you.' She swallowed hard. She hadn't meant to do this, had never intended to probe, but it was killing her, not knowing. 'What about you? Where are you going?'

'Admin,' Ciro started, then laughed at his own mistake. 'Ah, you were talking more of my long-term plans. Yes?'

'Yes.'

But Ciro didn't answer, glancing up at the sign above the door as they came to Maternity. 'This is you.'

'It is.'

And suddenly it was goodbye. The meeting would drag on for ever and her bag was over her shoulder so there was no reason at all to go back down to Emergency. No reason at all to prolong the agony a moment longer.

'If you change your mind about tonight...' Ciro started, but Harriet shook her head.

'I won't.'

A couple were coming out of the lift, the man calling urgently to them for directions as his wife limped along beside him, a pained expression on her face.

'Hold the door, mate!' he called, stress etched on his every feature, but his partner wasn't about to be rushed.

'Rex, we've got hours to go yet.' She managed a tired eye-roll at Ciro and Harriet. 'I wanted to stay at home, but he was getting that worked up.'

'Good luck.' Harriet grinned as they made their way past, but even the simple exchange took a mammoth effort. She watched Rex's arm wrapped protectively around his wife's thick waist as they made their way into the world of Maternity, and even though Ciro stood beside her now, smiled down at her with a look in his eyes she couldn't read, never had Harriet felt more lonely.

Ciro even held the door open for her, pushed on the black swing door and stood aside as she walked alone into the carpeted wards of Maternity.

And the irony wasn't lost on Harriet.

Seeing the signs for the birthing suite, baby photos lining the walls, the delicious milky scent of babies in the air, Harriet could scarcely fathom that in just a few short months she'd be here herself.

That one day or night in the not too distant future she'd be heading down this corridor just as she was now—excited and terrified and very much alone.

CHAPTER SIXTEEN

'YOU want the next floor,' Harriet explained patiently, before the stunning woman had even spoken, trying to keep the weary note from her voice as yet another of Ciro's ravishing sisters landed up at her door.

If the last two had been stunning, this one was gorgeous! Clearly she'd spent the day at the Alannah Hill boutique in Paddington.

Clearly, because a price tag was still attached to the top of the blouse, falling over her very impressive bosom. On any other woman it would have been the biggest fashion faux pas, but somehow it just added to her mystery. Her olive-skinned body was encased in pink ruffles, a massive fake water-lily adorned her glossy black hair and her impossibly skinny legs were strapped into the highest sandals Harriet had ever seen. On anyone else the ensemble would have looked like an over-decorated Christmas tree, but this feminine parcel, standing easily six feet tall, wore it all well, even, Harriet thought with an inward sigh, somehow managed to make it look understated. 'Dr Delgato lives on the fifth floor.'

'Oh, I'm on the right floor! You *are* Harriet?' she checked. Not waiting for an answer, she invited herself into Harriet's apartment. 'I have waited all day for you to come home. My name is Nikki.'

And Harriet could only rather reluctantly admire such confidence. Nikki hadn't actually needed an introduction and it had nothing to do with the process of elimination that this was the last of Ciro's three sisters and everything to do with her appearance.

After all, Spanish super-models weren't exactly hard to miss!

'You are nothing like I expect.'

'I'm sure I'm not,' Harriet answered stiffly. 'And now you mention it, neither are you. From Ciro's description I expected someone rather more…'

'Delicate?' Nikki finished for her. 'Oh, no!'

What she lacked in basic English Nikki certainly made up for in bad manners. Eyeing Harriet coolly, she sat down without an invitation and proceeded to light a cigarette. Harriet was damned if she was going to get her an ashtray, especially as she didn't even possess one!

Her steely resolve lasted about ten seconds. Rummaging through the cupboard, Harriet finally produced a saucer, but it wasn't entirely due to Nikki's rather intimidating stance—Harriet actually wanted to hear what she had to say and the diversion of producing a saucer gave Harriet sufficient time to drag the wind back into her sails before taking a seat on the sofa beside Nikki.

'So how can I help you?' Harriet ventured. 'Presumably you're here for a reason?'

'I want to see myself this woman who is too good for my brother.'

'I'm not sure what Ciro has told you…' Harriet frowned '…but our break-up certainly doesn't have anything to do with the fact that I think I'm too good for him.'

'Your job, then.' Nikki gestured to Harriet's rather drab-looking uniform, then dragged on her cigarette again, slanting almond eyes eyeing Harriet up and down. 'Your stupid career!'

As intriguing as this woman was, as much as Harriet yearned to glean any information about Ciro and his family, she certainly wasn't going to sit there and be insulted. 'Look, Nikki.' Harriet gave a tight smile. 'I don't know what's been said, and as far as I'm concerned it's none of your business, but for the record Ciro and I both decided this relationship was over. Both of us agreed that we wanted different things.'

'Your job,' Nikki said again, but this time Harriet shook her head.

'My self-respect!'

'What about my brother's self-respect?' Nikki demanded. 'My brother could be Chief of Emergency in Barcelona, my brother could be a Master of sports medicine, and instead he is talking about throwing everything away and staying in this backwater.'

'Hardly a backwater,' Harriet flared, gesturing to the gorgeous view of Sydney through the window. But her heart was hammering in her chest, her mind racing, trying to process Nikki's furious comments, trying and failing to keep a lid on the bubbling cauldron of emotions that was simmering inside her.

'Junior consultant in a suburban hospital.' Nikki somehow made the title about as appealing as working in the sewers. 'That is what you are prepared to reduce him to.'

Harriet had had enough. Whatever story Ciro had been spinning for his sisters, it was clearly so far removed from the truth it didn't even merit comment.

'I think you should leave now.' Picking up the saucer,

Harriet made a great show of flushing it down the waste disposal, flapping the air with her hands, but Nikki didn't give a hoot, tossing her hair and heading for the door.

'This you will regret,' Nikki said hotly.

'I doubt it,' Harriet answered tartly. 'By the way, you forgot to take the price tag off your blouse!' she added.

Nikki glanced down, a tiny arrogant smile forming on her pretty rosebud mouth. For a second she looked so like Ciro, it almost made Harriet want to weep.

'Oh, I did not forget, darling! As I said, I've been waiting for you so the boutique brought over a few items for me to try on. If Nikki can't get to Alannah then Alannah comes to Nikki…'

A second bang erupted just after Nikki slammed the door behind her—Harriet's shoe, spinning through the air and hitting the door—an attempt to vent the sheer frustrated rage coursing through her.

Damn Ciro and his bloody sisters. If she never saw another Delgato, it would be too soon.

So what was she doing, teetering along the ramp to the boat that was hosting Ciro's farewell party in strappy sandals and holding onto the captain's outstretched hand for dear life as she boarded? What on earth was she doing, dressed to the nines in a slinky black dress and not much else?

'Harriet.' Ciro was the first person to greet her, coming straight over, clearly delighted she had made it from the smile breaking out on his face. He dusted her cheeks with his lips, his hand warm around her waist, but as he pulled back, on closer examination Harriet could see the smile was strained, a thousand questions running through his dark, pensive eyes. But now just wasn't the time to voice them. Everyone wanted their last little fix of Ciro, and drinks were being thrust at him, toasts being made. As the boat started to pull away from the dock, Harriet gave him a tiny smile. 'You'd better get back to your party.'

'Later,' Ciro said. 'You won't leave without saying goodbye?'

'I'm hardly going to jump ship! Go,' Harriet added, grateful when Judith came over, beer bottle in hand and the smile of true friendship on her face.

'You look ravishing!' Harriet didn't even blush, just very glad that Judith was beside her, the one person she'd been able to confide in during these difficult times. 'Are you going to tell him? Is that why you came?'

'I don't know why I came,' Harriet admitted, taking a glass of orange juice from a passing waiter, watching the raucous emergency staff starting to party as only emergency staff could. 'I had every intention of staying home and watching a DVD when I met the third sister.'

'Had she lost her way, too?' Judith raised an eyebrow that had never met tweezers, and Harriet gave a low, mirthless laugh.

'I think Nikki knows exactly where she's going in life!'

'So what did she want?' Judith boomed, then grimaced at the sound of her own voice as Harriet shushed her.

'Who knows?' Harriet said bitterly. 'The way she was talking to me, you'd think I was the one who dumped Ciro. Does he look heartbroken to you?' It probably wasn't the most fortunate moment to voice that question because as the two women looked over they were greeted with the sight of Charlotte and Ciro doing a very strange version of the flamenco, being cheered on by the increasingly boisterous crowd. Harriet decided there and then she'd had enough. She wished now that she could jump ship, could just go back to her apartment and will the next few hours away. Telling Judith to cover for her, she made her way up the stairs and stood on the deck. She choked back jealous, angry tears, hating what she was reduced to, hating Ciro for the way he made her feel.

'I'll be down in a moment,' Harriet sniffed, hearing Judith clumping along behind her. 'Just tell them I'm enjoying the view.'

'A very beautiful view!'

The sound of Ciro's voice made her jump, and if there had been anywhere to go except the ocean floor Harriet would have stormed off. But instead she stood there, staring at the magnificent sight of Sydney Harbour at night, multi-million-dollar homes jutting out of the cliff face, anchored boats bobbing on the water and, tall and proud, overlooking them all, the opera house, its resplendent sails rigid in the wind. Even if Harriet saw it a million times, it was and always would be beautiful.

'Hardly a backwater!' Harriet said tersely, then checked herself, remembering it hadn't been Ciro who'd said it.

'You've been speaking to Nikki?' Ciro groaned.

'Actually, no, Nikki's been speaking to me.'

'Again I apologise. I do not know what has got into my sisters—I didn't even know they were coming.'

'Well, they're here,' Harriet snapped. 'And don't I know it. I don't know what you've been telling them, Ciro, but they're under the impression that I've left you heartbroken, that I'm not prepared to give up my career—'

'You're not!' Ciro broke in, and as her aghast eyes swung towards him his confident voice broke slightly, that beautiful full mouth struggling to hold it all together as he finished what he had started. 'And you have.'

'Have what?' Her voice was a mere croak.

'Left me heartbroken.'

'Ciro.' She shook her head in bewilderment. 'You're the one leaving, you're the one who said that you're not ready to settle down, you're the one walking away.'

'I have to, Harriet.' His eyes implored her to understand. 'I have worked all my life for this and finally it is happening. I have been accepted to study for a masters degree in sports medicine. It is the one thing I have been chasing for years and I understand why you don't want to move again after all you have been through, but please try and understand why I cannot stay. I have to go to Canberra.'

'Canberra?'

'The Australian Institute of Sport. I applied and never thought they would even consider me, but they wrote back...' Harriet thought of the letter he had hastily pushed to the bottom of the pile and closed her eyes in regret. 'They called me in for an interview. I wasn't going to say anything, thought it wasn't worth worrying you with something that might never happen. But it did.' He took a deep breath. 'Harriet, this is such an honour. I cannot believe I have even been accepted...'

'You're moving to Canberra?' If she said it again and he nodded, maybe, just maybe it could be true. 'You're not going back to Spain? But Charlotte said that you were, and Nikki said you were going to be Chief of Emergency...'

'Nikki has delusions of grandeur on my behalf, and as for Charlotte...' Ciro rolled his eyes. 'She has caused me enough problems.' His voice was serious now. 'Harriet, my sisters are worried about me, that is why they came. They decided to return the favour…' He smiled at her frown. 'Chocolate, red wine, a slushy DVD and, I am not too proud to say, many tissues…'

'Over me?'

'Over you, Harriet.' He took her face in his hands. 'The one woman who would make me throw it all away. My sisters have been trying to convince me otherwise, telling me that I am crazy. But, no, I say to them, I am just in love.' He stared down at her, utter adoration blazing in his eyes. 'I tried to make it palatable for you. When the job interview came up and I went to Canberra, I even stopped at the university and picked up some brochures on psychology. I thought maybe that would make you happy…'

'Canberra?' Third time lucky. The third time she said it, it actually sank in. 'But that's just a hop and a skip away. Why didn't you tell me? Why didn't you just ask me?'

'Because you had made it very clear that you were not moving again, and I understand completely. You had messed up your life enough, chasing Drew's career. I couldn't ask you to do it for mine. And then when the ANUM position came up…' He closed his eyes in bitter regret but Harriet's were wide open, seeing the past couple of months through Ciro's eyes, how difficult it must have been for him to broach the subject, to ask the woman he loved to give it all up for him.

Loved.

She did close her eyes then, as sweet realisation dawned.

This amazing, talented, beautiful man actually loved her—and she'd follow him to the end of the earth if she had to, live in a mud hut with two sticks if that was what he asked her to do. It had nothing to do with selling out or giving in, nothing to do with rewriting a promise she'd made to herself, and everything to do with the man staring down at her, holding her face tenderly in his hands.

'When you said you weren't ready to settle…'

'I meant here,' Ciro said. 'But if that is what will make you happy, Harriet, I will, without hesitation or regret…'

'There's no need,' Harriet broke in. 'Ciro, I don't want to hold you back. I want us both to move forward.'

'And we will,' Ciro said gently. 'Together, just us two.'

'Or three.' She screwed her eyes closed then felt his whole body become still as she not-too-gently dropped the news, bracing herself for his reaction. The heady feel of his lips on hers, the sweet, sweet taste of his mouth finally back on hers was all the affirmation she needed.

'Get a room, you two!' Judith boomed, making her way onto the deck and making them both jump. Ciro's arm was firmly around Harriet's shoulders as Judith made her way over briskly. 'What are you doing, man-handling my new ANUM?'

Oh, that!

Clearing her throat, Harriet felt Ciro's grip tighten around her as she let go of one dream to pursue another. 'Judith, would it cause a lot of problems if I pulled out of the ANUM applications?'

'Probably,' Judith said, but it was softened with a wink. 'Right now, I've got more important things to worry about. The captain's turning around and heading back to dock, he swears he's never going to let hospital personnel hire the boat again—and I wouldn't be counting on getting your deposit back, Ciro.'

'No worries.' He grinned, almost sounding like an Aussie. 'What the hell's that noise?'

'Charlotte!' Judith tutted, gesturing for them to follow and heading down the stairs to the party that was in full swing, Charlotte taking the microphone, eyes blazing, leading the crowd as a familiar song about survival, known to women the world over, started up.

Ciro smiled in delighted recognition, but his voice was suddenly serious. 'Do you think that Charlotte will be okay, I am worried that I have…'

'She'll be fine.' Harriet grinned, imbued with optimism for womankind as she felt Ciro's arm wrap around her. 'Just as I was—we're survivors!'

EPILOGUE

IT WAS nothing like Harriet had expected.

Even though they were in Canberra, even though one maternity ward was pretty much like another, walking along the corridors of the birthing unit was nothing like Harriet had anticipated. 'Lonely' wasn't a word that sprang to mind when a fresh batch of Delgato twins were about to make their entrance!

'Tell them to be quiet,' Harriet moaned, leaning against the wall as another contraction hit and Ciro energetically rubbed her back. All she wanted to do was go to sleep, all she wanted to do was climb into bed and rest a while, but the midwives were insisting that she walk around to speed things up. 'People will start complaining.'

'They're fine,' Ciro soothed. 'They're just excited.'

Excited didn't come close to describing the atmosphere in the waiting room. The television was blaring, the Delgato sisters chatting in their loud, expressive voices to Harriet's rather bemused mother, who was feeding lollies to Ciro's two thoroughly spoiled nieces, as Estelle happily and extremely competently breast-fed her twins at the same time!

And as much as Harriet adored them, loved them all,

suddenly all she wanted was for the noise to stop, for everyone to just go away and leave—even Ciro!

'This is all your fault,' she snarled. 'How the hell am I supposed to cope with twins?'

'I told you from the start that they run in the family,' Ciro answered easily, but his hand was waving for the midwife to come—preferably immediately!

'How am I supposed to finish my degree with two of them?' Harriet demanded, a complete alter ego emerging as they led her to the delivery room.

'You will.' Ciro was with her now, standing behind her and holding onto her forearms as she leant back into the welcome cradle of his arms, panic taking over as she realised that she wanted to push.

'They can't come in,' Harriet begged. 'I don't want anyone to see me…'

'Calm down.' Ciro's voice steadied her, a piece of driftwood in the turbulent ocean of labour, and she clung to it for dear life. 'Just go with it, Harriet,' Ciro said, his voice low and soft in her ear, and it wasn't annoying now, just everything she needed to hear. 'You just do what feels right for you and don't be scared.'

And she wasn't.

With Ciro next to her, Harriet could be who she was, pursue her own dreams and follow her own instincts with love always on her side.

'Clever girl!' Ciro's voice was louder now, urging her to keep going, to push just a little bit longer. 'It's got red hair!'

Which wasn't much incentive, but Harriet continued to push, screaming out loud as her baby slipped into the midwife's hands, hearing Ciro's joyous declarations as the angry pink bundle unfolded before her eyes, massive smoky blue eyes staring directly at Harriet. And she wanted so much to hold her, to relish the moment, but it was happening again, utterly no reprieve as her body continued its most important task. And it was just as miraculous as the first time, just as exhausting and exhilarating and as utterly amazing to bring her second child into the world.

'A girl!' It was Harriet calling it now, Harriet staring at the tiny bundle being swathed in wraps and handed to her as the first twin was brought back to join in.

'Two Harriets.' Ciro beamed, smiling and crying at the same time, staring at the angry little red-headed bundles.

Harriet didn't even mind when the entire waiting-room contingent trooped in. She watched her mother's face as she gazed in awe at her granddaughters, even managing to laugh when Nikki's petulant voice stated the obvious.

'More girls!'

'I am destined to be surrounded by women,' Ciro said proudly, kissing the top of Harriet's head, staring down at his brand-new family. 'And I wouldn't have it any other way.'

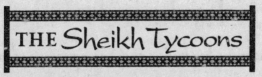

They're powerful, passionate—
and as sexy as sin!

Three desert princes—
how will they tame their feisty brides?

Layla Addison is powerless to resist Sheikh Khalil
al Hasim's wicked good looks, even if he's arrogant
and overbearing. But now he's demanding that the
feisty American beauty be his bride!

THE SHEIKH'S
WAYWARD WIFE
by *Sandra Marton*
Book #2774

Available in November.

www.eHarlequin.com   HP12774

HARLEQUIN *Presents*

Exclusively His

Back in his bed—and he's better than ever!

Whether you shared his bed for one night—
or five years—certain men are impossible to forget!
He might be your ex, but when you're back in his bed,
the passion is not just hot, it's scorching!

Things get tricky for sensible Veronica when
she unexpectedly meets Lucien again after one
night in Paris. And now he's determined to
seduce her back into his bed....

PUBLIC SCANDAL, PRIVATE MISTRESS
by Susan Napier
#2777

Available in November.

*Look out for more Exclusively His novels
in Harlequin Presents in 2009!*

REQUEST YOUR FREE BOOKS!

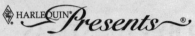

2 FREE NOVELS
PLUS 2
FREE GIFTS!

YES! Please send me 2 FREE Harlequin Presents® novels and my 2 FREE gifts (gifts are worth about $10). After receiving them, if I don't wish to receive any more books, I can return the shipping statement marked "cancel". If I don't cancel, I will receive 6 brand-new novels every month and be billed just $4.05 per book in the U.S. or $4.74 per book in Canada, plus 25¢ shipping and handling per book and applicable taxes, if any*. That's a savings of close to 15% off the cover price! I understand that accepting the 2 free books and gifts places me under no obligation to buy anything. I can always return a shipment and cancel at any time. Even if I never buy another book, the two free books and gifts are mine to keep forever.

106 HDN ERRW   306 HDN ERRL

Name _____ (PLEASE PRINT)

Address _____ Apt. #

City _____ State/Prov. _____ Zip/Postal Code

Signature (if under 18, a parent or guardian must sign)

Mail to the **Harlequin Reader Service:**
IN U.S.A.: P.O. Box 1867, Buffalo, NY 14240-1867
IN CANADA: P.O. Box 609, Fort Erie, Ontario L2A 5X3

Not valid to current subscribers of Harlequin Presents books.

Want to try two free books from another line?
Call 1-800-873-8635 or visit www.morefreebooks.com.

* Terms and prices subject to change without notice. N.Y. residents add applicable sales tax. Canadian residents will be charged applicable provincial taxes and GST. Offer not valid in Quebec. This offer is limited to one order per household. All orders subject to approval. Credit or debit balances in a customer's account(s) may be offset by any other outstanding balance owed by or to the customer. Please allow 4 to 6 weeks for delivery. Offer available while quantities last.

Your Privacy: Harlequin Books is committed to protecting your privacy. Our Privacy Policy is available online at www.eHarlequin.com or upon request from the Reader Service. From time to time we make our lists of customers available to reputable third parties who may have a product or service of interest to you. If you would prefer we not share your name and address, please check here. ☐

HP08R

HARLEQUIN Presents

EXTRA

MARRIED BY CHRISTMAS

For better or worse—she'll be his by Christmas!

As the festive season approaches, these darkly handsome Mediterranean men are looking forward to unwrapping their brand-new brides…. Whether they're living luxuriously in London or flying by private jet to their glamorous European villas, these arrogant, commanding tycoons need a wife…and they'll have one—by Christmas!

HIRED: THE ITALIAN'S CONVENIENT MISTRESS
by CAROL MARINELLI (Book #29)

THE SPANISH BILLIONAIRE'S CHRISTMAS BRIDE
by MAGGIE COX (Book #30)

CLAIMED FOR THE ITALIAN'S REVENGE
by NATALIE RIVERS (Book #31)

THE PRINCE'S ARRANGED BRIDE
by SUSAN STEPHENS (Book #32)

Happy holidays from Harlequin Presents!

Available in November.

www.eHarlequin.com

HPE1108

I ♥ HARLEQUIN Presents

**BROUGHT TO YOU BY FANS OF
HARLEQUIN PRESENTS.**

We are its editors and authors
and biggest fans—and we'd
love to hear from YOU!

**Subscribe today to our online blog at
www.iheartpresents.com**